People Can Change

People Can Change

D. M. Whitlock

Print ISBN: 978-1-7394137-2-9.

Published by Scripta Scripta.

For SW

Part One

Chapter 1
Death, taxes, and other people

LIFE, much like death, taxes, and other people, comes uninvited. It is thrust upon us, and one can only hope that some good comes of it.

Such was the case for Kate Harville, who, by the age of twenty-three, had weathered all such challenges.

Kate was the daughter of Cécile, an artist, and William, a small business owner. When William, still middle-aged, passed away, Kate grew close to her maternal grandmother.

For six years, Kate all but lived with her grandmother in Little House, a substantial building situated in the Midlands countryside, sitting on eight acres of woodland that was home to an army of squirrels, and three protected species (of which one was supposedly resident in the lake, though had not been sighted for some years).

The lake occupied three of the acres, and sat firmly in the middle of the woodland. Around it wound dirt paths, wooden bridges, and the occasional bench carved from a fallen tree. All created and curated by Kate's grandfather in his heyday.

As a young child, Kate's grandfather would take her on long rambles through the woodland. He taught her how to identify the various species of resident bird, insect, and fish, along with their Latin names. On quiet summer nights they would camp by the lake, cook over an open fire, and whittle soup spoons from softwood branches.

Some thirty years prior, Cécile enjoyed similar activities. Her father was more sprightly back then, of course, and would hoist her upon his shoulders whenever her young legs reached their limits. But no such luxury for Kate, who could only power through and hope, with time, to build resilience.

Kate's grandfather—Cécile's father—now gone, the woodland fell into an unmaintained state. The wood and rope that formed bridges was beginning to rot. Trees felled by high winds remained unmoved, obstructing paths. The paths themselves began to regrow vegetation from lack of human passage. To venture out onto the lake (once a regular weekend activity) seemed now to be a daredevil's errand.

But this was not a surprise to anyone. He had been the family's only naturalist, and the effort required to keep the woodland in a decent state was evidenced by his frequent, day-long maintenance treks. While his wife had been a teacher, and admired the nature which surrounded her, she held not the requisite skill or interest to tame it.

In her retirement, she taught classes at the local senior centre. But it was not a short journey, and when, after some years, it became impractical to continue, she turned her attention to Kate.

A social outcast, Kate became a frequent visitor, often turning up halfway through a school day. Her grandmother would welcome her with open arms, on the sole condition that she spend the time being homeschooled on 'things that actually matter'.

It was a mutually beneficial arrangement: Kate gained sanctuary from her educators and tormentors, and her grandmother gained company and much-needed help around the home. They became fast friends, beyond any sense of familial duty.

When, some time later, her grandmother passed away, the last thing Kate expected was to find herself named the sole beneficiary of her will.

It came as an equal shock to the family, and put Cécile's nose severely out of joint. Though she had never voiced her expectations aloud, it became apparent that, from a young age, she assumed she would inherit the family home. Perhaps it had been her retirement plan: a light at the end of the tunnel. And Kate had changed all of that.

The rift in the family was immense, and for twelve months immediately following the funeral, mother did not speak to daughter. So complete was the estrangement that Kate found out only from extended relatives that her mother had in that same period met someone and remarried: a well-to-do banker originally from London but now 'up north' after a promotion that saw him managing his own branch in the Midlands.

The pair endured an awkward encounter on the anniversary of the grandmother's passing, at the installation of her headstone.

'I can't believe you showed your face,' was the opening salvo from Cécile. 'After what you've done to our family. How you tricked your poor grandmother.'

The wind blew around them. In the chilly winter breeze, Cécile rearranged her scarf and pulled tight her coat. Kate's hair frolicked in the tempest. Her hands were plunged into her pockets, but she did not otherwise attempt to assuage nature's attack on her senses.

'It's nice to see you too, mother.' Then, turning to the man loitering nearby, 'And you must be my step-father.'

The man, Franklin, twisted his lips into a smile and nodded.

'Your mother and I felt it would be unduly disruptive to invite you to the ceremony,' he said. 'It was, after all, to be a day of joy and celebration. We wanted to keep drama to a minimum. You understand.'

Kate's eyes narrowed. She turned back to her mother.

Stretching to a seeming horizon (though in

truth, a mere dip in the landscape), markers of forgotten and soon-to-be-forgotten souls stretched in every direction. Some were brand new, shiny, and at odds with the field of decay they inhabited, but were destined to share the same fate.

'How considerate of you, mother. It's just a shame I couldn't have offered Little House for the wake— I mean reception. You know, there are so many rooms that just lie empty. It's quite the space for entertaining.'

That much was true. Even when Little House had been a family home, many rooms remained under dust sheet throughout the year, uncovered and cleared only when large functions or gatherings required the space. The wing of the house in which Kate now lived was nearest the entrance, consisting of rooms enough to sleep, relax, cook, and wash. The grand hall (for there was no better name for it) lay somewhere in the middle of the building, and had wide French doors opening out onto the gardens (which had also, sadly, fallen into an unmaintained state).

Cécile turned up her nose.

'It was you who set the tone of this conversation,' Kate reminded her.

'Fine,' Cécile conceded with a dissatisfied grunt. 'How have you been? How is Jane?'

Kate blinked.

'I'm fine.'

The wind picked back up, and Kate turned upon her heel, pacing away. For all that she knew, those might be the last words she would ever speak to her mother.

Jane was her oldest friend. They had always been, as with so many childhood friends, infuriatingly inseparable. In school they gossiped, and out of school they conspired to cause mischief. They were a permanent fixture at each other's houses, frequently sleeping over, copying each other's schoolwork, and playing rat-a-tat ginger on Sally Mason's posh parents.

In adolescence, life threw in their paths various upsets: Jane's parents divorced, and Kate's father suffered an untimely and fatal heart attack. The tragedies occurred within months of one another, and the pair counselled each other through their grief. But while Jane eventually adapted to her new normal, Kate struggled.

Education eventually—and thankfully—completed, they ventured out into the world and their relationship became strained under the sudden loss of proximity to one another. Kate found herself consigned to menial work in the face of a crass, unforgiving public, and Jane pursued a career in the arts, working as a museum assistant by day, and honing her artistic skills with classes in the evening. Jane's big dream was either to curate art, or to be an artist whose works were somewhere curated. It would be a long road to success, but if she failed it would not be for lack of trying.

Kate struggled to reconcile delight for the gradual forward progress of her friend's life with disgust at whatever god or force had decided to limit her own.

And so, when fresh tragedy created her the heir to a remote home and a small fortune, she quit the whole sordid affair and turned her focus inward.

Locked away in Little House, Kate spent much of her waking hours in deep contemplation of life. It seemed to be a wretched journey that bounded from one tragedy to the next, the path lined with the very worst folk society had to offer. She had received ill treatment from them all, and, formal education completed, had learned only a healthy suspicion of others' intentions.

Jane had also suffered from the slings and arrows of her peers. Even in the highbrow world of art and museums, the general public were not perfect. But with each year that passed, her empathy for Kate's plight became less and less effortless. When Kate committed herself to hermitry, the gap between their lived experiences widened, and the effort to empathise increased. As did the levels of persuasion required to coax Kate from her wooden haven.

Because Kate had decided: if the die was cast and she was to be forever tormented, then so be it; she would play the part and stay as far as possible from everyone.

Chapter 2
What is art, anyway?

IT HAD BEEN QUITE some time since Jane had last seen Kate. It was not a pleasure she could say that she missed.

It had become an effort to spend time with her old friend. Kate was prone to find malice in every interaction, no matter how banal. The occasional stranger whose furtive glance and subsequent laugh must have been mocking her appearance. The passerby whose shoulder collided with her own without apology. The one who said or did nothing at all, but by virtue of their resting expression or rancid cologne could be safely assumed to be a certain brand of nasty individual. Malicious, all.

But, on this particular day, the sun shining as it was, Jane was not thinking of Kate.

The gallery at which Jane worked was organising an exhibition, and it was time to start planning. With both of Jane's superiors out of action (a joint case of maternity *and* paternity leave, though pure coincidence and not in any way related), the question was posed to Jane:

'How about it? Do you feel up to planning the event?'

It was as big an ask as it was a privilege.

Of the event's success, she would not be accountable (that fell, as always, to the gallery owner). But for it she would be very much *responsible*. If the exhibition was a success, she could be sure to see new opportunities and responsibilities come her way.

There was much to be done.

First was the task of raising awareness. After all, the perfect exhibition would be all for naught if it was poorly attended. Then came the logistics of the night itself: how to greet guests, the efficient operation of the cloakroom, the serving of wine and hors d'oeuvres. The artist's appearance and speech was to be managed by the gallery owner, but their hospitality was likewise Jane's responsibility.

The enormity of the task loomed over her. She was thrilled and terrified in equal measure. Such an opportunity to prove herself! And yet such self-doubt in her ability to deliver. Perhaps, if she had been carrying out her duties for longer, she might feel comfortable. She was still the baby of the team.

'I'm worried I might make a mess of this,' she confided with her colleague, who at the time had one foot literally out the door, leaving on the last day before the start of her maternity leave.

'Good,' came the reply. 'Running an event like this is a big responsibility. People will be watching, and it will almost certainly impact your immediate career, one way or the other. So just remember that it's in your hands, and only you can make a success of. Put in the effort, go the extra mile, and it'll be fine. Now, I must be off.'

'Put in the effort, and go the extra mile...' Jane repeated to herself, now alone in the gallery. She looked all around her, slowly taking in the space that was for the first time her exclusive domain. It was hers to get right.

She decided to learn from the gallery's previous exhibitions. Poring over plans, attendance records, and sales figures, patterns began to emerge. When more wine was served, there was an uptick in on-the-night sales. When guest lists consisted of familiar names, turnout was higher. When guest lists were open to any interested party (tourists walking in off the street, for example), turnout was lower. Much of what she discovered seemed to be common sense.

But she also began to suspect that many of those responsible for organising previous exhibitions had not focused their efforts on the night's success. They were all artists at heart, and it seemed that, when given free rein to plan an event, it was viewed as a blank canvas onto which they could spill their ideas. Very few exhibitions bore structural similarities beyond the superficial requirements: art, drinks, people. Perhaps that was to be expected. They were art enthusiasts, not professional event planners.

And so, while Jane gathered information that *seemed* useful, the concern lingered: what if she went in entirely the wrong direction, or it all came down to nothing more than luck?

The sudden lonely nature of her job, and the scope of the task at hand, made Jane wish desperately that she had some help. Peers unavailable, she could only turn to friends for support. Luckily, she had one friend who knew a thing or two about art, and he worked just across the road.

Alex was a bartender at the Cock & Bull, the public house almost directly opposite Jane's gallery, and the drinking hole of local workers. Not quite the fancy wine bar Jane's colleagues might choose to frequent, but good enough for her to unwind after a long day of talking with members of the public.

In addition to tending the bar of the Cock & Bull, Alex was a failed artist, a lazy art lover, an avid rambler, and generally content with his lot in life. Like Jane, he too spent much of his day talking with members of the public, and in these interactions he witnessed the full scope of human drama and experience. In his moments of pretension, he would describe it as *Human Art*.

Most days on his lunch break, he would cross the street to peruse the gallery's works.

His philosophy on visual art was that there was always something new to observe. A good artist, he believed, did not create a picture in [figurative] broad strokes, but in the careful composition of its constituent parts. It was the juxtaposition of elements included, and equally the elements omitted. A single flick of paint (a silhouette in a distant window, perhaps) could radically alter the story being told. You could spend an hour taking in the details of a painting, stew on them for a week, and return with more questions than you started with.

At least so Alex thought. In creating such masterpieces of his own, he had been rather unsuccessful, abandoning his formal education in the arts after only a few weeks.

It did not take long for Jane to recognise from Alex's frequent and predictable visits that he was one who *truly* enjoyed art—that he never purchased so much as a giclée print was of no consequence.

She learned early in her tenure at the gallery not to presume the level of visitors' passion for art based on looks alone. The most smartly dressed and wealthy customers sometimes proved to have the least genuine interest, curating their collections as a signal of their wealth and status only. That wasn't what art was supposed to be about.

As she came to understand Alex's routine, Jane began not to ask whether she could offer him assistance, but instead to seek his opinion, and to share her own thoughts on those pieces he spent the most time admiring.

There was a certain impressionist piece they both rather enjoyed. It was painted in muted colours, and depicted rolling fields beneath a dark, threatening sky. On the horizon the sun—the work's only vivid use of colour—was setting, throwing golden rays onto the landscape from the far edge of the world. Silhouettes contributed further to the bleakness of the scene. Near the corner of the foreground: an outbuilding, with a grazing horse.

Jane shared her thoughts on the scene: 'A lot of people look first at the sun. Which makes sense; it's central and it's bright. But a sunset is also an everyday occurrence; nothing special, in many ways. But that horse... it's on its own. Is there a farm? A stable? What's just out of frame? How many other horses are there? Why has this one decided to brave the elements on its own? Is it waiting for something?'

Alex considered the observation. He drew closer to the painting and scrutinised the horizon.

'I think it's more about the break in the

clouds. Once you ignore the sun that shines through it, what you're looking at is stereotypical misery and gloom broken apart at its very heart. And a solitary horse is benefiting from that streak of warmth and light. What does that say?'

She chuckled.

'That we read too much into a pretty picture?'

Chapter 3
Up to the Fates

Before long, their mutual appreciation of art grew beyond Alex's lunchtime visits into something of a casual acquaintance.

Preliminary advertisements for the upcoming exhibition were now prominently displayed, including on the noticeboard of the Cock & Bull, and Jane's plans for the event were a frequent topic of conversation. Alex was her sounding board (though she had not told him as much). She would posit vague ideas to observe his reaction. And on some occasions she would plainly ask, 'What do *you* think?'

Her discovery process usually boiled down to the question, *Is there a right way to do this?*

It was perhaps more *philosophy* than *logistics*, and like art itself it often felt as if there may be no objective right or wrong. When the time came, would her research, hunches, and feedback sessions bear fruit? Or would the best laid plans fall flat under the unique whims of the day?

'I think you can only do your best,' was

invariably Alex's advice. 'And if there are setbacks, just keep trying. I think it has less to do with the individual things that do or don't go well, and more do to with showing up every day and trying. It's the end result you care about, not the individual successes or failures.'

'Perhaps,' Jane mused. 'What makes you say that?'

'The punters at the Cock & Bull. It may seem a bit old fashioned, but a lot of people who come for a drink at the end of the day don't come to get drunk; they come to reflect on their day. Over the course of months and years, you see patterns in people; their struggles at work and home. Even if the lows are really low, the effort can all pay off. The only ones that *never* have a happy ending are those who just give up and stop trying.'

'So success and failure isn't just with the gods?'

Alex shrugged.

'I think there will always be things you can't control. But that doesn't mean you can't course-correct after.'

It was not bad advice. It made eminent sense. But Jane could not help but think of her friend Kate, who fell very much on the opposite end of the spectrum.

Ever the pessimist, Kate had always found solace in understanding that life and the world would tend towards *not* favouring her far more often than it would. And in that state of being she was at least content in not being disappointed by the result of her efforts—it was easy to predict how horribly things would turn out.

To a point, their lives had progressed more or less in step with one another's. First young, then happy, then discontented, then suffering through tragedy. There was a lot of overlap. It was difficult to pinpoint the exact moment they began marching to the beat of different drums, but at some point Jane found it increasingly difficult to empathise with her friend's trials and growing sense of isolation. It was not that she *could not* empathise; more that their lives had diverged to the point that empathising required more conscious effort than unthinking reflex.

Because, for all she saw of her friend's continued misfortune, Jane's life and plans were actually progressing rather well. Although still early in her career, she had got her foot in the door, was doing something she loved, and on a daily basis felt the benefit of the professional inroads she was making.

To describe their relationship in perhaps the simplest terms: their shared experience of life had, at some point, suffered an insidious rift. *Not* thinking of Kate became an easier course of action for Jane than the opposite. She had effectively abandoned her friend.

Some of this she shared with Alex, their acquaintance now cultivated to the point of exchanging personal anecdotes and life stories.

Alex suggested that he understood, but Jane was not sure he really could. Those who insisted they could, rarely did. He was one of those individuals whose eclectic interests *should* render them an outcast, but instead enabled them to pass in most crowds without scrutiny. Perhaps a consequence of his chosen line of work.

Jane shared the history of her interest in the arts, and how it began at an early age. How, when teachers failed to nurture her growing talent and aspirations—and parents insisted that she instead focus on a 'useful' skill like mathematics—she honed her artistic skills in secret. How, for Jane, Kate would steal and deliver paintbrushes and tubes of paint from Cécile's studio. How canvases were more difficult to procure (and thereafter to hide), but how it was not an altogether *impossible* feat.

All roads seemed to lead back to Kate.

Kate was not a lover of the arts. Her adolescent passion had been in the night sky. She knew most of the constellations, and could point to and name the planets on any clear night. But school had likewise let her down.

Kate only engaged her educators once on the subject: in science class she raised her hand and asked when they would be learning about astronomy. She used words and phrases like 'nebulae', 'the Transit of Venus', and 'the Great Red Spot'. For her curiosity she was targeted by a fellow student with a sharp projectile, that collided with her temple, dangerously close to her eye. When laughter and taunting erupted amongst her classmates, the teacher chose not to quieten the class, punish her attacker, or enquire after her wellbeing; instead, she was told to leave the class for disrupting the other children's education. When Kate protested, she was threatened with further punishment, in the form of her classmates being kept back to do lines. Did she want to be responsible for that? Jane recalled her friend looking her classmates in the eye, one by one, before defiantly stating: 'Yes. Yes I do.'

From school, Kate and Jane learned a single valuable lesson: intellectual curiosity had no place in the classroom.

Jane promised her friend that, one day, when they were older, they would go on a trip to some remote, clear-skied region to take in the true splendour of the cosmos. That the excursion had yet to occur was one of Jane's deep regrets. But perhaps there was still time.

She had too many similar stories for comfort.

In a place of education that valued neither curiosity nor smarts, one could never be sure from behind which bush an aggressor would leap to inflict physical injury, or from which checked-out educator a lie or half-truth would be spread and twisted amongst the faculty, student body, and parents. If a child was the victim of particularly intense bullying, the playbook was not to deal with the culprits, but instead to carefully watch the victim for signs they might explosively fight back. Every wobble, every frustrated scream into the void, was subjected to scrutiny.

Adults had an odd way of framing the whole thing. The common refrain was, 'Things will get better when you are older.' (Though oddly enough, to those who did not suffer, the advice would invariably be, 'These are the best years of your life!')

The terrible truth was that, for Jane at least, things *did* begin to improve. With a passion to follow and a path towards it, she eventually found the company of likeminded individuals who nurtured her talent and encouraged her ambition. Little by little, she drifted from despair, and fought hard for a life that was, on balance, quite pleasant.

Leading such a different life, interactions with Kate became fraught with stress. To spend an afternoon with her, Jane had to prepare as though for a marathon. Her visits soon became less frequent.

It was sad. Jane missed her friend dearly, and mourned the loss of their camaraderie. She felt that, perhaps, she owed Kate a visit.

Chapter 4
Bearing the scars

'BE HONEST WITH ME... be honest with *yourself*. How long have you been tucked away here?'

Kate took a moment to consider Jane's question.

'Some measure of time,' she eventually replied. 'Perhaps only a few days.'

'Are you sure it's not weeks? Hell, it *feels* like months. Have you not missed being out in the world, knowing what's going on?'

Kate did not like this introspection. These were the norms of others: *go outside, see people, socialise with them*. But they were superficial. All one really needed was shelter and nourishment. Little House provided the former, and in the modern world the latter could be delivered straight to her doorstep.

Those were her primary needs; all else was optional. And that was just fine. Going above and beyond required other people. She had met other people—they were not the kind of folk she would rush to be involved with.

But why were other people so fundamentally awful? Although Kate considered herself to possess a reasonable intellect, the answer to that question was an enduring mystery.

As far as any objective witness could attest, she had grown up an average little girl. She had long hair, tied in plaits. She played all of the usual games. She wore the same uniform, bought from the same store, as those she learned alongside. She was, in most respects, entirely unremarkable.

Except there was something unknowable that marked her out to others. Was it the way she carried herself? The minutest of deviations in her understanding of the zeitgeist? Something rotten in her soul that permeated her aura? Whatever unknowable element set her apart, set her apart it did.

As a child, Kate did not have a dedicated tormentor. She instead found herself tormented by all: verbal and physical jabs; a years-long campaign to grind her down so in later life the lightest disturbance would blow her away.

She was not the only child to suffer at the hands of others, of course. But with her peers Kate felt little empathy. While they turned their sorrow to inward hatred of whatever unknowable trait provoked the malice of others, Kate turned outward with rage. That people so merrily embraced cruelty was a deficiency in *their* souls, not hers.

So went the lengthy exposition whenever challenged by Jane on her continued hermitry.

But Jane's purpose was to help lift her from despair, even if just a little.

'Why not get out and stretch your legs?' she suggested. 'You don't have to see anyone, but at least leave the house. Go for a walk to the lake.'

Kate murmured something that could have been dissent or agreement. It was cold outside, so she headed towards her grandfather's liquor cabinet, poured a sizeable shot of bourbon and swallowed it whole. Her insides suitably warmed, she braved the elements, exiting through the French doors of the grand hall.

The patioed floor gave way to a large garden, which had once been well-kept and neatly mowed. Now overgrown, in summer it presented as a pleasing meadow, but in winter showed its true, neglected nature. A stone pathway cut through the soggy meadow, leading to a gazebo on the right, and open woodland straight ahead.

The wind—if not the chill—abated immediately upon crossing the threshold between the garden and the woodland.

A well-trodden dirt path carried the rambler towards the lake. At this time of year, the lake was known to freeze over. A younger Kate had pleaded to skate upon it, but her grandfather was strict on the matter. Many years later she learned that, as a child, her mother made the same request, got out onto the ice, and when the surface gave way had almost been lost.

Kate followed the dirt path to the edge of the water. A pier, a dozen or more feet in length, and in severe need of maintenance, extended over the surface. She sat at its outermost edge and breathed deeply. Although still light, the moon was out in full force. Cold air coursed through her lungs. She closed her eyes and expelled a cloud of mist.

'Isn't this nice?' Jane questioned. 'It's good to get out of the house every once in a while.'

Kate remained silent, and continued to breathe deeply. She always liked this time of year. The cold air flowing into her body helped to ground her.

In times of anxiety, she often felt disconnected from the world. Sounds muffled. Time slowed and fractured, meted out in strobe pulses. She felt more an observer of her physical self than physically present. It was as though she were a kite flown by her inner self, her senses transmitted and dulled through the muted vibrations of the string that tethered her to her body.

It was the sting of freezing air in her lungs that could instantly bring her back into the here and now.

Kate opened her eyes. She glanced over the edge of the pier. Sparse patches of vegetation poked through. Just beneath the surface, something stirred.

'So,' Jane asked, 'do you think you can at least spend some more time out here? Just to get out of the house?'

'It is nice out here,' Kate mused. 'But I stay in the house for a reason; you know that. I'm alone there.'

'And you wouldn't be alone out here?'

Kate shrugged.

'There could be ramblers. Dog walkers. Idling youths. People are always where they oughtn't to be.'

Whatever had stirred in the lake now returned to its torpor, and the subsurface water was once more still.

Jane pressed: 'Perhaps. But that's no way to live. You can't hide away *just in case* you have an interaction with someone. Even if some people are rotten to the core, the enjoyment of a life fully lived surely outweighs the fleeting moments of misery and discomfort from a select few? And you seem to forget that you are a woman of means. You don't have to work. You have so much more control over your life than most people. You just have to put yourself out there. Meet some people and be friendly. Who knows; maybe they'll be friendly back?'

As the thought evolved and processed in her mind, Kate grew increasingly incensed. For a full minute, her angry stare pierced the distance. Sentiments of social experimentation concluded, she got to her feet and marched back to Little House, alone.

Chapter 5
Addicted to misery

A week passed. Kate hunkered down, and doubled her resolve to remain cloistered in Little House.

Making the house her own had been a slow process; changes were introduced little by little. Perhaps the most obvious addition was the bookcases that now adorned the walls of the living area. She found them, disassembled, in her grandfather's workshop—perhaps his last project before he died.

It took days to assemble them on her own, but the result was worth it: they were works of art; stained oak stretching almost the full height and length of the room. They soon came to house around a thousand books (some her own, but many gathered from other rooms in Little House).

The collection consisted primarily of the European classics, and Kate's interest in particular lay in the likes of Dickens, Hugo, Tolstoy, Dostoevsky, Austen, Proust, and Kafka, with the Americans Plath and Steinbeck thrown in for good measure.

Kate devoured literature in her seclusion, finishing the shorter stories in a single sitting, and tearing through the larger works in no more than a few days.

In eschewing the world she read deeply, and in reading deeply she eschewed the world. She identified heavily with Austen's heroines; the only sensible souls in a world of bumbling, selfish idiots.

It was difficult for Kate to measure the time between her interpersonal interactions in the traditional manner—minutes, hours, days, and the like—but she could recall the titles she had read in that same period. Since her last conversation with Jane, she had consumed six novels and three novellas. She was amid the final pages of L'Étranger when she was roused by a sharp knock at the door.

She tiptoed towards the door to peer through its window at an obtuse angle. Waiting for her were Cécile and Franklin.

A second thunderous rap shook the door in its frame. Startled, Kate jumped back.

'Open up, Catherine, your mother's come to visit,' boomed Franklin's voice.

Regaining her composure, she opened the door. Without looking at them or exchanging pleasantries, she waltzed back to where she had been sat.

The pair entered and followed her. Cécile trailed behind, taking in the alterations to the home she had grown up in. Most decorations and adornments remained as she would have known them, if not in the same state of cleanliness. The big addition was, of course, the bookcases. Positioned against walls that were previously bare (save for the floral pattern of the wallpaper and relief of the wainscoting), they were a towering presence. Franklin thumbed the shelf at his eye level.

'Think you can handle Ulysses?' he asked, pulling out the book and flipping through its pages.

Her private reflection complete, Cécile joined them in the room.

'Look, Catherine...' She wasted no time in getting to the point. 'Far be it from me to

32

interfere—you've certainly made clear your stance on being a member of this family—but as your mother I need to make sure you are okay. You've locked yourself away in this house, and it's not healthy. People talk, and it reflects poorly on all of us.'

Kate locked eyes with her, betraying nothing of her thoughts.

Cécile continued: 'Your situation... I need to make sure everything is...'

She was tiptoeing around something.

'Your mother is concerned that you've resumed your opium habit,' Franklin interjected, matter-of-factly.

'My what?!' Kate erupted, jumping up in astonishment.

'You know, dear, when you were about fourteen. You had those few months when you weren't quite yourself.'

'You mean when I was almost murdered? I'd like to see how well adjusted you'd be after something like that.'

'Oh don't be silly.'

Kate was fuming.

'Silly?! If it happened in the real world, someone would have gone to jail. But it was brushed under the carpet because "the police don't get involved in school matters".'—she gestured with her fingers as she quoted the officials who had heard her complaint—'Where do you get off inventing a drug addiction instead of supporting your child through trauma? You evil woman!'

As she became more agitated, Kate inched towards her mother, clenching her fists.

Franklin stepped between them. Though similar in height, he was nonetheless an imposing figure.

'You're getting hysterical. The fact is that your mother cares deeply about you. Too much so, if I'm being honest. You are an adult, but have achieved nothing, and just make excuses for yourself. By your age, I had a career; you don't even have a job. And more to the point: after all the misfortune she has suffered, your mother deserves to be happy. We are trying to build a life together, and her concern for you is holding her back. At the earliest convenience, I intend to move the family back to Islington.'

Back to civilisation, you mean, Kate thought. The words all but erupted from her lips, which bore the twisted, unmistakable countenance of disgust.

'But we cannot do that until you have grown up and your mother can stop worrying about you and your life choices.'

As he spoke, Franklin rested his arm on the bookcase he had previously been perusing. With his index and middle finger he wiped away a layer of dust, and with a flick of his thumb he cast it off.

Kate disliked him intensely.

It was not how he had injected himself into her mother's life, and how he now spoke for her that she disliked—that was Cécile's business, not hers. What she disliked was the familiarity with which he spoke to *her*. He did not know her at all. And yet, in the few minutes of their lives they had so far shared an acquaintance, he had managed to land insult after insult, each delivered as though they were on intimate terms.

She disliked how, even in the bosom of her solitude, these people could emerge to drag her into an invented family drama. And she disliked how *blood*, for some inexplicable reason, linked her to them forevermore.

Family and belonging was a topic Kate used to enjoy debating with Jane. In a post-agrarian society, she pondered to what extent *belonging* was a meaningful concept. The survival genes that led people to say stupid things like 'blood is thicker than water' didn't seem all that beneficial in a world that ran so completely on individualism. How cruel, she would argue, in such a world, to demand familial obedience after inflicting the trauma of being plucked from the void and cursed with sentience.

'So, it's decided,' Franklin stated quite abruptly; 'you'll get your act together, get yourself a job, and grow up so your mother can move on with her life.'

'Excuse me?' Kate objected.

Unflinching, she stared at him. His expensive clothes and an apparent life free of consequences did not impress her.

'He said, dear...'

'I know what he said, mother. The problem is, I don't respect your boyfriend here. Nor you, for that matter. To come into my home, state boldly that my life is worthless, and demand I act a certain way to further his aims? You're as selfish as each other.'

'We just want what's best for you,' Cécile pleaded. 'I won't have you throw away your life after I worked so hard raising you. You used to be such a pretty girl when you smiled. You used to be so full of promise...'

Before Kate could respond, Franklin offered once more his thoughts: 'Believe it or not, young lady, your mother and I don't just have a few grey hairs for our age. We have a lifetime of experience. The time for stubborn idealism has long passed; you need to sort your life out.'

There was some truth: Franklin and Cécile did indeed have a few grey hairs. But only a few.

They resided alongside Cécile's mop of chestnut brown, and Franklin's sea of white.

Kate marched away.

'You can both leave now,' she called to them.

The conversation was over.

Chapter 6
Rambling on...

THE SUN HAD SET and the moon cast long shadows in the garden. Her eyes closed, Kate relaxed on a reclining chair. She was outside, enjoying the sounds of the night: the rush of the wind and the chorus of a hundred crickets.

After some time in a deep meditative state, she was wrought to alertness by the unexpected snap of branches. All manner of scenario raced through her mind. Foxes and magpies were frequent visitors, but the distinctive snap of wood underfoot could not be their doing. Somewhere, not too far off, was an intruder.

Kate rose to her feet and unleashed a guttural demand: 'Get off my land!'

The fury in her voice was not an act. She was terrified and incensed in equal measure. Closing in on her might be someone intent on causing her harm.

The trespasser—whoever they were—had but a moment to decide their bravery. Would they dare to persist and discover who screamed at them so fiercely? Or, having been discovered, would they flee?

Further branches creaked and snapped. Kate held her ground. From her pocket she retrieved a set of keys; they would serve either to get her quickly to safety, or to dispatch the stranger who crept steadily towards her.

Against the backdrop of tall trees that abutted the garden, a silhouette formed. Its features were ill-defined, and remained so as it marched forward.

With not a single polite word, Kate once more screamed at them. This time, the intruder came to a halt. They raised their hands in surrender, and continued to approach at a slower pace.

'I'm sorry,' they called, in a voice strong enough to carry over the distance of the garden. 'I didn't realise this was private property. I was just out for a walk. I got lost on the trail off the main road. I thought this was all woodland.'

'It is,' Kate replied in a no-less-threatening manner. She continued: 'The woodland is mine. There are fences; you must have jumped them. Now turn around and leave!'

'Wait...' said the stranger, taking a single step forward. 'I didn't mean to trespass. There was a gap in the fence, I thought I was still on the trail. I passed a lake and benches.'

Kate did not say a word. She took a few more steps, but the face of her unwanted visitor was still obscured by shadow. She could only tell that it belonged to a man who was in his twenties or thirties.

'I'm Alex,' he offered, hands still raised in surrender. 'I'll go back the way I came. I'm so sorry to have startled you. I hope you have a good evening.'

'Fine. Now be gone!'

'And... and you are?'

'Maggie,' Kate lied. 'Now get the hell off my land.'

'Hello, M—?'

From a deep, restless slumber Kate was awoken by the clang of her door knocker. She rolled over and sharply recoiled as the sun cast

its wretched splendour upon her face. Though
her eyes could not yet focus, from the intensity
of light she reasoned that it must have gone ten
o'clock.

She rose, pulled on a gown, and groggily felt
her way to the front door. Her eyes still not
entirely open, the knocker sounded again.

'Hello, Maggie?'

'Wrong house!' she groaned, turning to find
the nearest soft surface on which to collapse.

Again, the knocker sounded.

'I'm sorry to disturb you again,' the caller
said, just loud enough to halt her retreat. 'I
stumbled into your garden last night. I hope you
don't mind; I just wanted to apologise properly,
and to show you where the fence was broken, so
you can get it fixed.'

From somewhere in the depths of her
drowsy mind, Kate managed to recall the
previous night, and the false name she had given
to her intruder.

Still half-asleep, she had yet to regain the
composure and clarity required to make clear
her position on strangers at her door. She was
also in no mood to entertain someone who
clearly could not take a hint, having already
trespassed on her property once under cover of
darkness, and seeming content to continue
doing so now in broad daylight.

Groaning, she stumbled back to the door,
cracked it open, and leaned her face into the
frame.

The morning air crashed upon her cheeks,

waking her just enough to be able to say, 'Alfred. Whatever twisted sentiment you have contrived, just go. I turned away those missionaries, and I'm turning away you.'

'But your fence...'

The door slammed shut. Kate wandered some twenty feet and crumpled onto a sofa, resuming her slumber.

Some hours later, she was jolted awake once more, this time by the tug of gravity that, after some tossing and turning, had wrenched her from the sofa and brought her to a swift meeting with the oak floor.

But for the occasional variety in the hour she woke, Kate's morning (sometimes afternoon) routine was predictable. Breakfast was a quick affair, consisting of buttered toast, a bowl of oats, and a glass of orange juice. The grain calmed her gut, and the juice provided the energy to prepare for whatever the day might require of her.

She sat reclined in a chair. In her left hand was propped a novella, and her right hand alternated between a slice of toast and a glass tumbler.

Before long she was sated; both her hunger, and also her curiosity about the fate of her latest story's tragic heroine. As she read the final chapter, she waltzed towards the kitchen (focused entirely on the book in her hand), to discard the used breakfast implements. Her wandering took her close to the entrance of the grand hall. Catching sight of the garden through its French doors, the events of the previous night and of that morning surfaced in her mind.

'The nerve of that rambler...' she muttered, as she at first recalled his excuses, and then felt anxious over his attempted re-intrusion into her home.

She raced into the grand hall to seek assurance that she had indeed locked the doors, and peered into the garden to check that it was empty. She repeated this at the front door, peering through the window and cracking the door just enough to observe that all was well. The area immediately beyond her front door was clear, and the sun still being out offered some assurance that, were she to leave the house, she would be alone.

She slipped on a pair of flat shoes and took a

tentative step outside, musing, 'I need to fix that fence...'

She remembered that her grandfather kept tools in the huts.

The huts were small brick buildings dotted throughout the woodland, built by her grandfather for the purpose of storing whatever tools he regularly required to maintain the woodland. Beyond axes, Kate was not sure what she might find there, but she assumed some other useful tools must be present. Most of the huts were along the beaten path, though Kate had discovered at least one that was isolated by a crop of sapling growth. It would take the axe that the hut surely contained to clear a path to its door.

Wandering into the woodland, she found the nearest section of fence and followed it in a clockwise manner. With the hindrance of mud and uncontrolled vegetation, a walk around the perimeter could take up to twenty minutes.

After a few minutes, a figure came into sight: a man. Although he was turned away from her, Kate could see that the stranger held a section of the fence in his hand, which he promptly tossed aside. Another trespasser! Had she been but a minute earlier in setting off, she might have witnessed the act of destruction itself.

She instinctively dropped her posture and crouched out of sight. A deep frustration and sense of anger and fright again coursed through her, as hushed obscenities leapt from her mouth.

She slowly crept forward, in an attempt to improve her vantage point, but a twig snapped beneath her foot. The stranger stood up straight, and stared menacingly into her soul.

Chapter 7
Things to be fixed

Kate cowered, turning away and searching desperately for something she could use to defend herself. But there was nothing to hand; only the clothes on her back and the twigs on the ground.

As the stranger approached, she turned back. The adrenaline was pumping, but the all-important *fight or flight* decision had yet to be made. She rose to her feet, clenched her fists so they could aid in either hitting or running, and... stopped.

Her terror turned rapidly to confusion and anger, as the *latest* trespasser upon her property continued to advance upon her and revealed himself to also be the *last* trespasser upon her property. There stood the interloper who called himself Alex, manhandling the very fence he had boasted of scaling the night before.

'Maggie!' he exclaimed with alacrity.

Kate emitted a shrill scream. It was the kind of scream that, in her most helpless dreams, produced no sound, breaking through only at the height of her most desperate anger, and for all her efforts producing only a muted hiss. But here it escaped in full force. She threw her clenched fists to the heavens, like a child mid-tantrum.

'Why won't you leave me alone?!' she cried. 'Why can't people just leave me alone?!'

Alex once more held up his hands in surrender.

'I'm sorry,' he offered. He sounded like a broken record, and Kate had little patience for hollow apologies. He continued: 'I just wanted to fix the fence so others wouldn't make the same mistake. After the fright I gave you, it really felt like the least I could do. The work was simple enough: a post had dislodged, and some of the wood had rotted. It's nearly sorted; I just need to reattach this last piece of wood to add some tension, then I'll be off.'

With haste he made the final repair. It did not excuse his repeated encroachment, but the visibly rotting wood at least convinced Kate that he had told the truth about how he came to be on her land. He had also carried out the bulk of the work in her absence, which somewhat confused matters if he were up to no good.

But Kate knew that a kind act was never free. In her youth, she was befriended for the benefit of her smarts, or as a scapegoat for the mischief of whatever group had adopted her. In her retail work, those who shopped with a smile would often see fit to scream, shout, and insult when their pleasant demeanour did not afford them a steep discount. And when protected from the general abuse of one stranger by another, the latter would invariably expect her company as recompense for their good deed.

In a world where accidents and selfless acts simply did not exist, she pondered what motivation lay behind her strange series of interactions with this Alex.

'What's your game?' she, to that end, demanded.

'I'm sorry?'

'You. Knight in shining armour. What's your game? Did you break my fence just so you could fix it?'

Alex stuttered as he replied: 'No. I... I just felt bad. It was easy to fix, and you seemed so unhappy with me this morning. I thought I'd just fix it quickly and be off. My good deed for the day, you know?'

Kate's eyes narrowed. She looked him up and down. There had to be something he wanted. People just didn't do things like that. Every act had *some* motivation.

'Well it wasn't for you to fix,' she eventually told him. 'I didn't ask you to, and I didn't need you to. You're a perfect stranger; you ought to stay out of my way.'

He closed some of the distance between them and offered a further apology: 'I'm sorry. It's just the kind of person I am. I like to fix things. And I felt awful about last night. I wanted to do something to make it up to you. The fence seemed like the obvious choice.'

As he spoke, he leant on the freshly fixed section of fence, and promptly recoiled in pain, clutching one hand in the other.

He had become impaled on a nail protruding from the surface of the post he had just re-set. An initial trickle of blood flowed across his palm and down his middle finger, dripping upon the leafy floor below.

Kate failed to suppress a delighted cackle. She did not rush to his aid—the injury was *his* folly, not hers. But as he cast incredulous eyes upon her, her delight in his comeuppance softened. A grimace was the best response her face could now offer.

At a distance, she instructed him to elevate his hand, and asked what item of clothing he could sacrifice as a bandage. The arm of his overshirt sufficed. Tying it tight around his hand, the bleeding was stemmed, at least for now.

Silence passed for some time between them. Eventually, he sighed and looked around.

'I can't believe this is all yours,' he commented. 'It's really quite beautiful.'

Kate nodded. It was. It had been even more beautiful in earlier years, when her grandfather was still around to look after it. Under his stewardship, the paths were clear, stray branches trimmed back, and the fence strong. It occurred to her that only she and her mother now recalled the woodland's former glory.

'I'm not much of a gardener,' she admitted. 'It used to be better cared for.'

Alex looked around once more. He breathed deep through his nose. The sun was low in the sky; its light penetrated the canopy at sharp angles, casting long shadows.

'I quite like it as it is,' he commented. 'It's beautiful. Like art.'

Kate rolled her eyes.

'Art...'

'No, think about it. Everything has a story. That tree with the scar from a missing branch; what happened there? When did the lake form? What lives in it? All these stories, they're art. Just no one's painted them yet.'

'Art...' Kate repeated her dismissal, with a tut.

'You don't like art?'

'Let's say I don't. Why, are you some kind of artist?'

Far from discouraging him, Kate's response seemed to empower Alex to launch into the tale of his failed life as an artist. He told of his fledgling talent, his abandoned education (on that subject, Kate chuckled), and the good fortune of working opposite an art gallery. It was here that Kate learned that he was a bartender at a public house called the Cock & Bull. On the subject of his love of art, it all sounded rather banal.

He spoke at length and digressed often. Kate found her attention drifting. She thought of Jane, and how she used to talk in a similar manner. Quite unlike Kate, she was one of those people who could see things that weren't there. But it had been a long time since her friend shared with her her passions. Kate wondered whether, perhaps, she was somewhat at fault. As Alex continued his animated discourse, a single tear crept down her cheek.

'Maggie, what's wrong?'

He shifted forward, reaching out with his bloodied hand.

She dabbed away the tear, and scowled at him.

'Never you mind. And it's—'

She caught her words and held them back. In reminding her of her dear, old friend, Alex had created a sense of familiarity that now made her uncomfortable. He already knew where she lived and how she behaved under stress—that was concerning enough. Getting on a first-name basis would be a bridge too far. *Maggie* she would remain.

'It's none of your business,' she recovered, then turning on him: 'Anyway, what's *your* deal? Honestly? Are you some relentless Boy Scout who never grew up?'

Alex chuckled and began to collect his things.

'No. But I should be off. This has been an interesting experience. The fence is fixed now, so next time I'll just knock on the door.'

Next time? Kate marvelled.

He continued: 'There's an art thing soon. A friend of mine is running it. You should come. There's a painting that has *you* written all over it.'

Kate pulled a face; a most unconvincing smile.

'No thank you.'

'Don't just say "no"... think about it. It's good stuff. You might even enjoy it. In fact, I think you positively will.'

'I'm saying "no",' she replied. 'I don't go out. There's nothing good waiting for me in a crowd. And you're just the latest in a very long line of people to try to convince me otherwise.' She was now in the midst of a well-rehearsed and oft-repeated speech. 'And don't insult me by suggesting I've just not been to the right places or met the right people. Every idiot says that. Every idiot thinks they're the one who can fix me. I don't need fixing.'

He seemed unfazed. Normally Kate's

monologue at least caused frustration in its recipients. He was a perplexing one, to be sure.

'Drop by the Cock & Bull some time, then,' he said, having already turned from her and begun to walk away. 'I can promise at least one friendly face there. Bye, Maggie.'

Part Two

Chapter 8
Demanding a favour

FOR THE NEXT TWO WEEKS, Kate remained holed up with her creature comforts inside Little House. Her reclusion was punctuated only by the regular delivery of essentials to her door.

The folk who delivered to her had, over time, come to know something of her. Most knew her as the hassle-free customer who was prompt in opening the door and accepting the goods without idle chitchat—ideal for those overburdened with deliveries. But some, presumably with more time on their hands, would attempt to engage her in conversation. These were her least favourite type of person to find at her door.

While the happiness of strangers was not her responsibility, she knew she could not be unduly rude, as they provided a service she very much needed to continue uninterrupted.

She thought of the advice Jane might offer (she had been doing this increasingly), and found that just the right level of engagement—

basic pleasantries and little more—could end an awkward and unwelcome conversation in an acceptable amount of time. On disengaging such people, she became quite practiced.

Other visitors were less manageable. Once more, Franklin led the charge, with Cécile in tow.

His plans to remove the family ('the family', of course, referring only to himself and Cécile) to London had hit somewhat of a stumbling block. Whatever arrangement he thought he had reached with the top brass had evidently not, in fact, been reached. It would be necessary to win the good graces of his superiors. These were men who could decide his future with the swipe of a pen. He clearly would give anything to become one of them. But they were infuriatingly out of reach to those such as poor Franklin, who languished in the provinces. Politics and nepotism were, as ever, alive and well.

Such was the earful that Kate received as Franklin, quite uninvited, paced around her house, expounding his woes.

There was only one solution, he explained: a number of the men he needed to impress were soon to be in the area, overseeing the launch of a new branch, and he would take the opportunity to throw a soirée to remind them of his name and his competence. His banishment would end.

For the gathering, he explained that he needed two things: a space to host the event, and to show that he was a trustworthy family man. For the latter, a wife was a nice start; but a dutiful, well-mannered daughter would seal the deal.

'You don't have to speak to anyone,' Cécile assured Kate.

'In fact,' Franklin quickly clarified, 'it would be better if you did not. You don't even have to smile; just spend an evening not looking so gloomy. I will introduce you to three very important men, and you will curtsy. You will then stay out of the way, and by the end of the night I will have secured the support I need.'

Kate was at a loss for what to say; there were so many intense thoughts and feelings to express, all fighting to get out. That her family saw fit to use her for their own purposes, without so much as *asking*, should not have surprised her. But surprised—amazed—she was.

Words still absent, but evidently on the tip of her tongue, Franklin said, 'What is it? Come on; spit it out, girl.'

Before she could erupt into her usual fury, Kate once more thought of Jane's calming voice, and the advice she might offer.

Just smile through one night, help them disappear to London, and never see them again, was the advice she imagined she might receive. It was just the kind of advice her old friend would offer. And though the implications for her were infuriating, Kate could not deny that it would at least forever remove the blight that was her immediate family.

It took all of her strength to agree to play her part. She did so without smiling, and with (as

Cécile commented), 'much huffing and puffing.'
But she agreed. One night, and she would be
free of them.

Agreement to attend the soirée and play the
dutiful step-daughter secured, then came a
second request, not from Franklin, but instead
from Cécile. The request, of course: to
commandeer the grand hall of Little House for
the event.

'It is what your grandmother would want,'
she assured Kate, taking it upon herself to
unlock and enter the space.

She glanced every which way, tutting and
commenting on the cobwebs that draped the
corners of the wall adornments and various
pieces of furniture.

'Is there a problem?' Kate demanded. Could Cécile *really* not put her compulsion to criticise on hold for long enough to ask a selfish favour? It was beyond comprehension.

'Well, it's just how neglected this place has become, my dear. What would your poor grandmother think? Her precious home! She would be turning over in her grave.'

The fact was that Kate's grandmother had been complicit in the deterioration of the place. She had been too old to get into the nooks and crannies, Kate had been too lazy, and between them it never once came up in conversation.

Of course, Kate felt bad that she was not staying on top of things, but she would not be made to feel guilty by her mother in her own home. She may have neglected the house, but to her grandmother's health and immediate needs she had been dedicated beyond reproach. It was a time during which Cécile was largely absent, and any memories she professed to have were likely to be imagined. Kate had been there, and her memories of the time were not of the decor, but of tragedy unfolding in slow motion.

Cécile continued: 'Yes, it really is a shame. You should take better care of this house, if it is to be yours. You need to dust, and you should get someone in to do the rugs—they look rather shabby.' And then: 'Are those mud prints?! Oh, Catherine, really!'

'Out!' Kate demanded, pointing to the door.

'Now see here,' Franklin interjected.

'Out!' She screamed. 'You can host your party elsewhere.'

The pair stood before her with their vapid, stupid faces, unmoved by her demand. An air of expectation lingered. In frustration, she grabbed one of her grandfather's hand-carved antique chairs, and upturned it. An almighty clatter echoed throughout the grand hall. Splinters flew past her, and with a stamp of her foot and point of her finger she reiterated her demand.

'Why, you ungrateful little cow!' her mother shouted. 'When you know how much this means to the family! That you won't share my own home with me for just a few hours! You wicked child! I obviously did a poor job of raising you, if this is how you treat me now. No wonder you don't have any friends!'

In an ideal world, such comments and

accusations would not have caused Kate any pain. In a *fair* world, those who insisted on being so cruel would have no means of gaining an audience with her. But in the real world, they did, and they had. Kate found herself quite impulsively taking Cécile's bait, reverting for the briefest of moments the role she despised the most: *child*.

'I have friends!' she barked.

'Do you?' Cécile scoffed. 'Making people up now, are you, Catherine?'

'My name's Kate! And if you must know I made a new friend last week, so don't you worry about me. You live your life, and I'll live mine. The sooner you disappear to London, the better.'

Cécile began to sob.

Kate shook her head and laughed. She knew that sob. It was textbook *Cécile who isn't getting her way*. It was emotional blackmail, plain and simple. But Kate had dealt with blackmail before, and she knew not to engage. Cécile actually made it easy: the heartstrings she imagined she was tugging on had long ago snapped.

'Now you've upset your mother!' Franklin barked. He put his arm around Cécile, supporting her in her imagined frailty, and made for the door. In their wake, he dropped the words, 'Don't worry, Sissy, we'll find another way. We'll leave your daughter to her miserable life.'

For a full twenty minutes after their departure, Kate's heart galloped. The unwelcome intrusion and insults replayed in her mind. As resolute as she had been—as firm as she ever stood—she had been unable to muster any authority to which they would bow, or even to grudgingly respect.

It took a week for her anger to subside, and only then could she revisit their selfish request. She made a decision: to be rid of them once and for all, she would lend her home and play the dutiful daughter. It was a decision she was opposed to on almost every level, except that, once suffered, she would finally be free.

Chapter 9
The Cock & Bull

IT WAS nothing short of an emergency that required Kate to venture out: when her weekly grocery delivery failed to arrive, she found herself embarking on a trip to the high street to buy some essentials.

It was a quick shopping trip, and the day now saved, she hurried home. But mere moments into her journey back, one of the bags split, dashing the contents across the pavement. In frustration, she dropped the other bag and screamed. She was still twenty minutes from home, and there were too many items to carry in her arms.

She curled her fists tightly at her side and threw back her head. Closing her eyes, she forced herself to breathe deeply, counting aloud in time with each breath.

In her frustration, she considered abandoning the scene of the crime and returning home. The street around her was certainly not cared for by others: discarded food wrappers, spilled food and drink, and things she chose not to identify were abound. In just the few moments it took her to make this observation, she witnessed two passersby spit on the floor. What would be the folly, really, in contributing her own filth, when others seemed not to care one jot?

It was not something she would normally consider; that behaviour was the remit of others. And yet, she found it increasingly difficult to hold herself to higher standards when she was the only one. Clearly no one else cared, either to refrain from littering, or to condemn it when it occurred.

Before she committed to an action, one way or another, she felt a tap on her shoulder.

'Maggie!'

Oh hell, she thought.

Slowly opening her eyes and levelling her head, she found Alex stood before her, grinning like a fool.

'What the hell do you want?' she snapped.

He adopted a muted smile and glanced at the mess surrounding her.

'Do you need some help? I can fetch some bags.'

'You just happen to be here, when my bags break? And have replacements ready for me? What are the odds?'

He shrugged. 'Quite high? You chose to cause a scene outside my workplace.'

To her left, Kate saw the old wooden beams of the Cock & Bull. A wooden sign hung beside the door. It was in the shape of a bull, with the shape of a cock deftly cut from it—a silhouette within a silhouette. It hung from two rusted chains, swaying creakily in the breeze.

Kate had never been inside, but she was familiar with the building. It was one of those old buildings that public houses invariably occupied. Once upon a time a private house, now likely a listed building, and laying claim to some dubious credential like *the oldest continually used building in the country.* The door led to a long corridor that stretched the length of the place. The bar was located at the rear, and every few feet gave way to a door (or at least a door frame) that opened up into a snug.

From inside, someone called to Alex. He was needed back at the bar.

'Look,' he said, 'I have to get back to work.

But I think we have some bags behind the bar, so give me a second and I'll fetch them for you. I've got a break in ten minutes, so why not gather your things, set yourself up in the front room, then I'll buy you a drink, and you can tell me your woes?'

She would rather be at home, but her feet were starting to hurt, and she was currently in no mood to lug everything back.

After rebagging her groceries, Kate settled into the frontmost snug. It was the only room with windows, and consequently the only one that received any real amount of natural light.

The snug was not all dissimilar to a small room at Little House she had recently converted into a reading nook. There were wooden benches with dirty cushions, crooked wooden tables, creaking wooden floorboards, and in one corner a roaring fireplace. It was a lot of wood around an open fire, but evidently the adjoining rooms were similar, and the place had yet to burn down.

The building as a whole was surprisingly quiet, and rather empty. Kate recalled seeing some advertisement earlier in the day regarding a sporting event, so it was possible that the local club were busy playing their rivals from the next town over, and the quaint, cramped public house had therefore been emptied of its patrons.

Kate placed her shopping bags on the floor, and sat on one of the benches. She produced a small book, Vladimir Nabokov's *Pnin*, found her place, and began to read.

She had managed no more than three paragraphs before Alex entered the room, carrying in each hand a glass of some dark-coloured drink.

'I didn't know what you wanted, so I just played it safe,' he said, passing her one of the glasses without hinting what it might contain.

She placed the glass on the table, sat upright, and dropped the book into one of the bags. Alex, now seated, looked at her. Just what was he expecting? Gratitude, most likely. But for the bags? The drink? Providing her with company during his break?

'Mm,' Kate grunted, signalling a gratitude as ambiguous as the act for which it was warranted.

He made some small talk. Her replies were

terse, and her body language decidedly uncomfortable, but he seemed not to notice—or, perhaps, not to care. He asked about her outburst on the street, and commented how fortuitous it was that her disaster occurred where he could be of assistance. What a set of remarkable coincidences that their paths had once more crossed!

Kate nodded and contributed the bare minimum to each conversation. He spoke in quick succession of the kismet of their continued meetings, art (and the event he again insisted she would enjoy attending), and literature.

It was only this last subject on which she perked up and felt ready to contribute more than the bare minimum. Literature was something she lived for. Was there any chance that he, too, was an avid reader? That might make him not entirely uninteresting. When he enquired what book she had been reading, he commented in return that he had *War and Peace* at home, sat on a shelf.

But their discussion was cut short.

Through the window, two people came into view: Cécile, with her face all but pressed against the glass, and Franklin by her side.

Seconds later, the pair were in the room, keen to understand what they had happened upon.

Chapter 10
Kate, in context

'I DON'T BELIEVE IT... you were telling the truth; you really did make a friend!'

Such were the words with which Kate was greeted by her mother. Clutching her handbag to her front, she eyed Alex curiously. Franklin stood behind her, but his attention was not in the room.

Alex glanced at Kate. His eyes asked the obvious question: *Who is this? And why are they looking at me?* By way of reply, Kate offered only a close-eyed exhale.

A proper introduction not forthcoming, Cécile demanded one directly: 'Don't be so rude. Who is your friend?' And after a prolonged silence, 'I asked you a question, C—'

'Alex,' Kate quickly interjected. 'This is Alex. He works here.'

'Alex...' Cécile mused. 'Nice to meet you. I've heard all about you.'

Her hand moved slightly, as if to offer a handshake, but no sooner had it shifted than it retracted back to her purse. Her attention turned sharply back to Kate, who was quite unsure who to focus on or what to say. Or whether to speak at all. Would they all just go away if she said nothing?

Cécile wasted no time in filling the silence: 'I'm glad to see you making friends, my dear. Heaven knows you've had a hard time keeping them. You must remember to be kind to this one. You're a grown up now, after all.'

Franklin concurred: 'Indeed. Though at your age you should be focused on building a career and securing your future.'

Kate scowled.

'I agree, darling, but we must make allowances for those who have fallen behind. How can she expect to keep a job if she can't make friends and smile every once in a while?'

'Of course!' Kate replied, locking eyes with her mother. 'I must learn to smile before I can learn to be obsequious. Big smile, red lips, brown nose!'

A splutter of laughter erupted from Alex. He attempted—unconvincingly—to mask his mirth with a cough, but not before drawing everyone's attention. As Cécile and Franklin took their turn to scowl, Kate took hers to smile.

She was keen to be rid of the pair. Their presence, as always, was unwelcome, and if they divulged her real name she would have one more mess to clean up. She could imagine her mother's condescending tone, scolding her for 'making things up', and questioning why she 'couldn't just be normal?' Conversations she had no patience for.

'Alex here only has a few minutes before his break's over,' she said, placing a hand on his arm. 'So if you'll excuse us, I should spend the time practicing how to be friendly.'

Cécile narrowed her eyes. Franklin's gaze was cast across the street, where the small branch of a rival financial institution was situated.

'C—'

'You can have your party at Little House,' Kate interrupted. 'My outburst the other day was— Well, warranted. But you can use the house.'

Franklin's attention was now focused entirely on those in the room.

'Excellent!' he said, with a clap of his hands. Now that he was on the brink of getting what he wanted, he was fully engaged. 'Your little friend should join us. It'll be good life experience for the both of you; you can see how business is conducted.'

Their needs satisfied, the pair said a quick goodbye and made a hasty exit. Alex watched them through the window as they marched down the street and turned a corner.

'Wow,' he commented. 'You know, I think I understand.'

'Hmm?'

'You. That. You grew up with them...'

Kate slumped forward. The exchange had sapped all of her energy.

She shook her head and shrugged.

'To an extent. Cécile's on form. But Franklin is a recent addition. I don't know how permanent a fixture he is. Not that I much care. He wants to move them both down to London, and he needs my house to impress people so that can happen. But good riddance. I hope he succeeds.'

Alex nodded his head as though he understood the situation.

'So I'm not the only unwelcome visitor to your home?'

'Bingo,' she confirmed, with a point of her finger. 'You've hit the tip of the iceberg.'

She preferred not to waste much energy discussing her family. Superficially, it was nice to be empathised with, but it was infinitely preferable to just not speak about them. Alex, she was now sure, felt sorry for her, and companionship is no companionship at all if it comes dripping in sympathy.

She thought about her family often, though. She wondered at what point it had all gone wrong. Cécile wasn't always intolerable—Kate thought that at some point she may even have been loving. Surely, when the world first turned against her daughter, some part of Cécile's heart must have broken? To see the girl who used always to smile adopt an unending frown, returning home day after day with tears in her eyes, scrapes on her limbs, and letters from teachers questioning what must be so very wrong with her for the other children to be so *unusually* cruel.

The empathy, if it had existed at all, was short-lived, and Kate's primary memory of her mother during that time was of disdain for her reluctance to *just be happy* in the face of the daily verbal and physical abuse.

When, in the workplace, it seemed the norm for colleagues and customers alike to seek to undermine her credibility and sabotage her livelihood, Cécile's attitude had long been aligned with that of her educators: that there must be something rotten in her soul to attract so much negativity from those around her. Why couldn't she just change, for her own good?

Kate was deep in contemplation when Alex spoke up to address the lingering elephant in the room.

'Sorry if I misheard, but did your mother say she knew who I was?'

A grimace took ahold of Kate's face. She once more squeezed shut her eyes and breathed deeply.

She answered in a calm, measured tone: 'It is possible that, in anger, I invented a friendship to win an argument. That you actually exist in real life is coincidental. Though quite useful, as it happens. But she is also lying, as usual: I said nothing about you other than *you exist.*'

Alex nodded in understanding.

'In any event,' Kate said, 'your break must be over. Thank you for the drink.'

❧

Alex's break was not over. His morning shift had concluded, but he was not due back behind the bar until later in the afternoon. And he saw no better way to spend his time than getting to know Maggie. She was in *his* world now, and the strange interaction with her family had only made him all the more curious. He was somehow caught up in a web of lies, and he was curious why.

He fetched for her a drink of her choice; a hard liquor so infrequently requested that the bottle was coated with thin layer of dust.

As she drank, she opened up. Where she had previously been a woman of indeterminate grunts, facial winces, and expressive eyes, now she was a measured conversationalist. While details might not be readily forthcoming, he could at least infer them from what she did *not* say.

He inferred that the relationship with her surviving parent—the woman she would refer to only as *Cécile*—was strained, and that she held the uncanny ability to get under her skin. On the subject of her father, he could learn nothing. Of her step-father, she was vocal and unrestrained. He learned the finer details of Franklin's ambitions, and his tactless demands to requisition her home and trot her out like a show horse.

When she was angry, Maggie spoke at length!

As she spoke, he wondered about her. She was one who carried a fiction book when out shopping, and who perked up when the topic of conversation turned to literature. That was surely a passion he could relate to: a love of imaginary worlds and the interpretation of what the artist had created. Jane had taught him to consider what lay beyond the bounds of a painting—as an avid reader, Maggie would likewise surely read between the lines to invent the million nuances that would make her stories come to life.

They conversed for well over two hours. The frozen items in Maggie's bags began to melt. They tore through a variety of bar snacks, and several more drinks. When it was time for the third round, Maggie volunteered for the first time to pay for and fetch the drinks. She then turned the topic of conversation on Alex, shooting his probing questions right back at him.

One question was rather pointed: 'What horrific thing happened to make you so sociable? No one is this cheerful. Not really. What are you overcompensating for?'

He was unsure how to respond. He had his stories and triggers like everyone else, but he never felt that he overcompensated or was overly friendly. He told her as much, but from her twisted lips and scrunched-up face could see that she was not convinced.

When the time of his afternoon shift drew near, their parting proved awkward. Were they now acquaintances? Friends? Alex was not sure, so simply reiterated his former offer: there was an art exhibition soon, and would she like to attend?

She shrugged off the invitation, but in a

welcome surprise invited him to Little House, to help her dust off the cobwebs and prepare the place for her step-father's party. 'Since you like to fix things.'

With an awkward handshake that almost became a hug, they parted ways.

Chapter 11
Clearing away memories

CÉCILE WAS, in Kate's esteemed opinion, not one for objective truth-telling. She viewed the world through a twisted lens that distorted what was right in front of her, and was not afraid of sharing her biased opinion. But on one subject, at least, she had made an astute observation: the grand hall was not presentable, and the spiders had well and truly moved in.

In many ways, the space reminded Kate of her school's assembly hall. From the wooden block flooring, to the high windows that required a special pole (whereabouts unknown) to open and close, it was awfully familiar.

Scattered throughout were numerous dining tables and chairs. They had not been used since the room's last gathering, a decade or more ago, and remained in the same positions they occupied when the tired, unfulfilled promise of 'we'll tidy the room tomorrow' was uttered.

The tables could be dismantled, and this was the first task Kate set about. She would move them to a corner of the room, and then stack the chairs along the far wall. Again, reminiscent of her old school's assembly hall. She knew that in one of the living areas she could find her grandmother's antique room dividers, and thought she might use them to obscure any untidy areas that remained.

She remembered playing with them as a child. Her grandfather would sometimes use them to create a small maze, and give chase as she zigzagged through it. He was masterful in his pursuit, menacingly appearing from behind the last corner just as she was about to turn the next.

But Cécile was not a fan of such games. Kate recalled her criticising her father, saying, 'Really dad, don't encourage her! She's excitable enough. All this nonsense is no good for her.' But he would always continue, undeterred. Some further words would surely be muttered, but amid her squeals of excited fear, Kate could never make them out.

Cécile viewed childish fun as the progenitor of adult wickedness. When Kate found a marble in the gutter and took it home to play with, she was loudly chastised for all the items she would undoubtedly and illicitly 'find' later in life, and be made to feel guilt over the people she would be depriving of them.

But from Cécile, affection and kind words could be bought with an apology.

'You won't be a bad little girl any more, will you? Of course you won't. You want to make your mother proud.'

It became worse as she grew older. In adolescence, Kate deviated so rapidly and frequently from Cécile's ideal that they barely spoke. Cécile made a show of being exasperated. She just could not understand her daughter or her morbid outlook on life.

'Why can't you be like Sally Mason? She's just like you, but *she* doesn't get bullied. I can't imagine what you must be doing to set off the other children.'

Sally Mason's mother seemed to be everything Cécile aspired to. She was a strong, confident woman whose child never spoke back. She was a solicitor, and by the age of thirteen and a half her daughter was on track to follow suit.

Sally Mason's parents would orchestrate lavish birthday parties for their daughter, and they would invite her entire year group, Kate included. One year, around the age children begin to learn from adults that they should not automatically like each other, Kate was dropped off, present in hand, and edged her way towards the other children. But they did not acknowledge her, and at the behest of Sally Mason turned away to snigger.

For three hours, Kate observed the fun from a distance.

There was another quiet little girl lingering at the edge of the action; a girl named Jane. Over their shared exile, the pair became immediate friends, and spent those three hours learning everything there was to know about each other. But when Cécile returned to collect her daughter, she cared only for the report from Mrs Mason that Kate had not taken part in the activities—that she had been naught more than a wallflower.

The admonishment was predictable: Kate had been invited to a party, but had failed to embrace the social event with open arms; what on earth was wrong with her?

As her work on the tables progressed, Kate found that she had reached the limit of what she could achieve on her own. A few of the tables were partially dismantled, and the chairs around them collected in low stacks, but it became obvious that she was attempting a two-person job.

She perched upon one of the chair stacks and wiped her brow. She had worked up quite a sweat.

From this vantage point she could see straight out of the French doors. After a short while, she saw Alex emerge from the woodland and traipse through her garden.

Cheeky bastard couldn't use the front door... she thought.

Soon enough, his face was pressed against the glass as he waved. He probably couldn't see her, because when she moved forward into his field of vision, he jumped back in shock.

She motioned for him to step back, and opened the doors out into the garden. Although it was a chilly day, she left them open to give the dusty old room an airing.

'Say, this is quite nice,' he said as he gazed about. In the room before him were fine tables and chairs, imposing pillars, magnificent windows, and a large grandfather clock. 'I understand why you like it here.'

'You don't have the first idea why I like it here,' she retorted, but in his wonderment he may not have heard her

They exchanged basic pleasantries, and she set him to work. Between them, they soon managed to dismantle and move all of the tables. Then began the lengthy job of stacking the chairs.

An hour of hard work passed. They had made a decent dent in the chairs, but still had many more to tackle—they were not designed with *stacking* in mind.

At some point in the second hour, they began to converse. Just enough to make the work feel less tedious.

Alex asked about the room they were in, and Kate tersely relayed what she knew of its history. It had been somewhat of a multipurpose room. In decades past, it had hosted everything from dinner parties to small concerts. It was, ironically, often used for exactly the kind of event that Franklin had now requisitioned it. The part of the building that it occupied had been built by a great, great-great, or great-great-great relative, who was some kind of industrialist with an obsession for extending the family home. *Little House* had, originally, been an apt name for the small cottage that now had what might reasonably be called *wings*.

'That's incredible. You're very lucky to have a home like this. Did you inherit it from your grandparents?'

'Mm...' Kate grumbled. 'Cécile did *not* like that. But she wasn't the one looking after her mother those last few years. I didn't expect to get this place, but I'll be damned if I didn't earn it.'

Without prompting, she began to rant about her mother and her various cruelties; how there was nothing quite like being gaslit by a human whose biological *and* legal job was to protect you and prepare you for life. It was difficult for Kate to convey how completely unsupported and sabotaged she had felt—there were few events of significant magnitude that would make others understand; it was instead a life of constant paper cuts, grinding down her resolve to continue just showing up every day.

Alex did not understand. The look on his

face told her as much. It seemed to say: *Bad things happen to everyone. So what?* But it was so much more than that. Widening her complaint to society at large, Kate spoke of a pattern of behaviour: strangers bumping into her and pushing her out the way; mothers screaming at her for *their* child's bad behaviour (when a child once toddled up to her and punched her hard on the leg, a profanity slipped from her mouth and the child's mother threatened her with physical violence); co-workers stealing her possessions... as one-off occurrences, they would be unfortunate, but these were things that happened *every day*. And it was far from an exhaustive list.

'It's just your face,' her mother had once told her. 'You choose to go out into the world with that look. It invites the disrespect of others.'

That might have been true. But if she appeared so sour to others, it was not for lack of a reason. Besides, should she have to shape her aura—or whatever resting features and body language people mistook for an aura—for the benefit of perfect strangers? It was absurd.

'There's a lot there I can't relate to,' Alex finally admitted. 'But I get the existential stuff. I think everyone can relate to that. Those deep, philosophical ponderings about ourselves. In some ways, it's like ar—'

'Don't say "it's like art"...' Kate interrupted. 'Not everything is art.'

At this, he fell silent and sulked.

She frowned. She expected a bartender to have tougher skin.

'Don't be an idiot,' she scolded him, then sidled up beside him to deliver a short, sharp punch to his upper arm. 'Smile.'

'Wow. It's almost like you *care* about me,' he replied. A whisper of a smile crept onto his face. 'Almost like I might just be your friend.'

'Please don't use the *F* word around me.'

Chapter 12
Making progress

THE CLEARING of the grand hall of Little House began on Saturday and did not end until Sunday. The initial *to-do* list—moving furniture and dusting the fittings and fixtures—did not take much time. What kept Kate and Alex busiest was the litany of secondary tasks they uncovered: cleaning the dust that was somehow caked onto surfaces, reaching the highest cobwebs, polishing fingerprints off mirrors and other shiny surfaces, and washing a decade's worth of bird droppings from the windows (some, also, entirely out of reach).

There were points at which Kate felt overwhelmed and considered giving up. She could down tools, send Alex home, and tell Franklin to find another patsy. But when her energy and enthusiasm flagged, Alex was there to offer encouragement and make a game of ticking off the remaining tasks. He reminded her how it was all building towards her ultimate goal: to be left alone, at long last.

The conversation between them came in fits

and starts. There were some hours during which they said nothing to one another.

But a bond was developing, regardless; the bond of two people, stuck together in an increasingly futile race against the clock, to complete some mammoth task that ultimately served to achieve someone else's goals. For a brief moment, Kate understood workplace camaraderie: it was an artificial affection to help people cope with wasting their precious time for some person or cause they didn't much care for.

She had yet to determine what Alex wanted from her. He had now helped her on a few occasions, and had yet to attempt to claim his reward. It frustrated her to not know what he sought. If she understood his motives, she could prepare to handle them. But he just continued working hard, smiling at her, and making intermittent small talk.

When he spoke, he was more guarded about his life than he evidently expected her to be about hers. He had a skill for asking just the right questions to set her off on lengthy diatribes on the subjects about which she held strong opinions—likely a skill he had honed in his work behind the bar. She tried to play the same trick on him, asking similar probing questions in a similar tone and manner, but the result was not what she hoped. Perhaps she could not fake the extraversion required. Or perhaps he did not value others' private lives as he did his own.

She found out the basics. Of his family? He had one. Of his upbringing? It had not been smooth. Of his exhausting positivity? He would at least concede that it was a conscious effort to pour more positivity into the world than he received.

Perhaps he believed in karma.

Whatever the reason, he was intent on being decent and helpful. And if that meant he could help her be rid of those who were decidedly *not* decent and helpful, she would make use of him, like a snake unleashed to tackle an infestation of mice.

On Sunday, when Alex dutifully returned, they turned their attention to the surfaces. For hours they mopped the floor—a thankless, backbreaking task that was not as quick or as easy as it first appeared. It also proved to be hazardous. They both slipped on various wet patches; only too late did they realise the folly of not working from back to front. Making matters worse, the cold climate did little to speed the evaporation of the water, and when it eventually did evaporate, the windows became misted, highlighting fresh areas in need of cleaning.

But, by the end of the day, the grand hall felt every bit the space for people to meet, converse, and engage in soulless pleasantries with each other.

Earlier in the day, a note arrived from Franklin, outlining the plan for the event. Wine and hors d'oeuvres were to be served. He would hire the requisite staff, and they would arrive early enough to set up. A gardener would also visit, to tidy and clear the space at the front of the house. With the help of a colleague back in London, a painting of the man he hoped most to impress would be borrowed and displayed prominently in the grand hall. If necessary, wall fittings would be added for the painting to hang in a suitable location.

Kate gritted her teeth. Why did she continue to bow to her family's wishes? She could only remind herself of the payoff, and of how many hours remained until both the start and the end of the ordeal. It was survivable.

The work finally over and Alex departed, she sat alone in the large, cavernous room, on a single chair directly below the chandelier that had been far too high to dust.

She was exhausted. For some time she stared idly outside, enjoying the cool evening breeze as it swept through the open doors.

It had been some time since she had last seen Jane, so she was surprised when her friend appeared.

'This looks nice,' Jane said, commenting on the neat and tidy grand hall. 'You do all this by yourself?'

Kate shook her head.

'I had help. Do you remember that trespasser?'

Now Jane shook her head.

'Someone broke in?'

'In a manner of speaking. He more *waltzed* in than anything else. The nerve of strangers! And now he's trying to help out and be my friend.' She stopped to think. 'Wait— how long has it been?'

Jane shrugged.

'You're making a new friend, though? That's encouraging.'

'Encouraging?!'

'I just mean, I can't be your only friend.' Kate locked eyes with her, but she continued: 'It's good you're opening up to other people, that's all. Talking to only me can't be healthy.'

Kate chose to ignore that last comment. She then mused on the subject of *Alex*.

'I must admit, he has been helpful. Even if he *does* ask too many damn questions. Truth be told, if it wasn't for him, I might not have had the motivation to see this thing through. Imagine it: once they're in London, I'll finally be free! After I also see *him* off, of course. But that shouldn't be too difficult; he doesn't have his claws in yet. Just think: no more interlopers!'

'Mmm...' Jane grumbled. 'Maybe you should focus on exploring this new friendship and drawing people closer, rather than devising ways to push them away?'

But this plea did not land. *People* were far and away the primary cause of pain in Kate's life. As benign as Jane's advice might have seemed, it was an invalidation of every lived experience that had shaped Kate's harsh stance on people, acquaintances, and their impact on her emotional wellbeing. It was, effectively, an instruction to lower her guard that ran contrary to the defences she had carefully—and from necessity—built up over the years.

'I don't expect that kind of nonsense from you,' she scolded her friend. 'Of all people, you should know. You know I'm right. *Friends make you happy* is one of those lies adults tell children.'

'Is that how you feel? Thanks.'

And at that, Kate was once more left alone, to stew in her own thoughts.

Jane had changed, and Kate did not like it. Her life had taken a more fulfilling route, laden with friends who had not yet made her feel completely awful about herself. Good for her. But Kate would not be guilted into treading beyond her comfort zone. Not even for friends, new *or* old.

What would become of her acquaintance with Alex was yet to be decided. Maybe they would continue to bump into each other, and form some attachment. Maybe she would come to depend on him. And maybe that attachment would, some months or years down the line, gut her completely.

It was not beyond her ability to make friends. But she knew too well the cost of letting people get close.

As she gazed at the night sky, she wondered when she would next hear from Jane. Her visits had become less frequent and more ephemeral. Were the last remnants of their friendship slipping away? And had it all been her fault?

Chapter 13
Building castles on quicksand

ALEX'S BURGEONING acquaintance with Maggie continued some days after they finished clearing the grand hall.

He appeared at her door with a polite knock, and, after some convincing, was invited inside. They re-inspected their work, and he took the opportunity to ask more about the upcoming event. After yet more convincing, she eventually relented, cracked open a bottle of whisky, and started complaining about her step-father.

He chuckled as she handed him a whisky glass that was close to overflowing; she would make a terrible bartender.

He took small sips—spirits were not his drink of choice. But Maggie knocked back two glasses in a row. It was almost comedic. Almost.

As the alcohol worked its magic, Alex observed how freer Maggie became with her words. He saw this every day, of course. But he could not help but smile as it happened to *her*. He found increasingly that when he asked her a question, a straightforward answer would be forthcoming.

Over the course of a few short hours, she became animated, angry, upset, overjoyed, and more. She *really* did not like her family, and from what he could understand of her childhood, it almost made sense. She told stories of the children she grew up with, and he was torn over whether or not he believed them. He did not *think* his new friend Maggie was the type to fabricate events and the people responsible for them, but some of the cruelties she described were hard to believe. He assumed a sober retelling would be more palatable.

When it came time for him to head to work for the evening shift, Alex found himself accompanied by a very drunk Maggie.

She hung off the bar—in a quite literal sense—while he worked, alternating between talking at him and ordering more drinks to stave off sobriety.

At some point, the busiest part of the evening came to an end. Those who needed soothing after a hard day's work had been soothed, and only the usual barflies remained. Until now, Alex had not been able to pay any attention to Maggie, and at some point she had disappeared. But now all was quiet, she returned, and he greeted her afresh.

'Hi Maggie!'

She looked at him gone out, before declaring: 'Who's Maggie?— Shit, shit. *I'm* Maggie. You don't know my secret.'

She attempted to order another drink, but

he declined to serve her; she had had too much to drink already. He did not drink much himself, and found he was not pleased to discover that his new friend might be one to drink to excess. Had she been drunk that first night they met, when she screamed at him like a banshee?

He sensed her agitation at being refused, and attempted to change the conversation.

'What do you think about the art exhibition? Do you think you'll attend?'

He pointed to the open door. Through it, the gallery front was visible, lit up like a Christmas tree.

Maggie shook her head, smiled, and laughed.

'No thank you.'

'Are you sure? You should go; you'd like it.'

She once more shook her head.

'No.'

'Not even for your new friend?' he joked.

To that, Maggie's reaction was unexpected. Her demeanour soured immediately, and with language he had not heard even from her, she emphatically decried: the event, his invitation to it, and his 'continued inability to respect [her] boundaries'.

He was taken aback. Not so much by her words, but by the intensity with which she delivered them.

'Maggie, I don't understand... what's wrong?'

She scoffed.

'Maggie! You don't even know who Maggie

is. Why do you even *want* to know Maggie? Is she just someone for you to fix?'

'I—'

'She is *not* a toy for you to insist on appearing here or there, to do what you wish, and be thankful for the privilege!'

Alex reached out in an attempt to calm her down. Something was clearly bothering her, and he didn't want her to cause such a scene that his colleagues might try to eject her from the premises. He found her hand, which she promptly snatched away and swung at him. He leaned back, but not quite far enough to avoid enduring some minor injury. One of her fingernails caught his nose and drew a speck of blood.

He grabbed a towel and dabbed at it.

He was not shocked, or even angry. She was not the first person at his bar to take a swing at him, and she would not be the last. He just stared at her plainly, waiting for her comedown and the inevitable moment of self-reflection. Through experience, he found that not reacting to an attack was often the quickest way to prevent it escalating.

But her rage did not subside. She breathed heavily, shoulders rising and falling, eyes peering out from beneath her brow. She grabbed a glass, held it high, and with a shrill scream smashed it down on the bar. This attracted the attention of several of Alex's colleagues, who emerged just in time to witness her exit the building, a trail of blood marking her path from the bar to the door.

❧

Kate strode away without looking back. She could feel Alex's presence some distance behind her, and suspected that he had followed her at least part of the way down the high street.

The blood continued to drip from her hand.

As she turned the corner, the Cock & Bull and Alex's precious art gallery disappeared from sight. She looked behind her, to catch the precise moment they disappeared. Good riddance.

When she turned back, she found that she was face-to-face with someone. She instinctively lurched back, stumbled, and managed to right herself only by leaning on a wall, where she left a bloody handprint.

Before her stood Jane. She wondered why she should see her *here*, and not at home, as had become their custom.

Jane looked her up and down.

'You've really done it this time, haven't you?'

'What?' Kate asked, bemused.

With a nod of the head, Jane hinted first at Kate's bloodied hand, and then at the handprint on the wall.

Kate held her hand to her face, so close that it blurred before her eyes. As she moved her head back it came into focus, and she could see for the first time the deep cut on her palm. She could not see any glass in the wound, but it was bleeding profusely.

'What happened?' Jane asked. And then, as Kate continued to wobble, 'How much have you had to drink?'

Kate sneered.

'Kate!'

'Fine. Fine! You want to know what happened? Faced by the relentless onslaught of social obligations, I cast off both the shackles of my polite soul and the pretender who sought to claim a stake in my life.'

'How eloquent.'

'Thank you.'

'And then?'

'Then words failed to convince, and I smashed a glass.'

'Mm. And was it worth it?'

Kate thought for a moment. She had

declined Alex's invitation a number of times. And after each rejection he produced another reason why she should change her mind. It was not enough for her to possess a valid reason for her decision—she must have failed to appreciate what was on offer!

So was it worth it? She rather thought it was. She knew what came with the territory she had charged into: the label 'hysterical'. But it was a rare day that such an outburst did not do the trick. Sober or otherwise.

The blood that still dripped from her hand had attracted the attention of a few worried bystanders, including one police officer doing his rounds. Spotting the bloodied, stumbling, and not-entirely-coherent woman, he raced to her and asked if she was okay.

Kate turned to look at Jane. 'More bloody help I don't need.'

'I think you might need this help, Kate,' Jane said.

'Here, let's get you over to that bench,' said the officer. He steadied Kate and walked her to a grassy verge across the street. 'Can you tell me what happened, miss? You seem to have quite a nasty cut there.'

'Just ask my friend. As they're *so concerned* for my wellbeing...'

'Miss, I need *you* to tell me what happened.'

Kate sighed, groaned, grunted, and threw back her head all at once.

'That bloody bartender,' she mumbled. 'Wouldn't take *no* for an answer and insisted I came with him. Why don't they ever listen? I was practically kicking and screaming!'

After some coaxing, the police officer was able to record the basic details. He saw to it that she was seen by a doctor, who was able to clean and close her wound. The cut was short, but deep—almost to the bone—and may have severed some nerves. She was told that she might lose some dexterity in the hand, or suffer a loss of sensitivity in some of her fingers.

Throughout the whole ordeal, Kate was stoic, betraying nothing of her inner thoughts.

She recalled the events of the day and their swift escalation. Had she overreacted? Perhaps. She wondered if events would have unfolded differently had she not been drinking. But did she regret standing up for herself, even now she knew the bloody cost? She thought not!

For better or worse, she owned her actions, and made no apologies for them. Her shortcomings—whatever they might be—were the product of her experiences, and her virtues survived in spite of them.

She mused over people, and the strange norms they tacitly agreed to. There was a point beyond which most people would not stray: to break social etiquette; to stand upon tabletops, and shout profanities; to flagrantly fail to recognise figures of authority within family, society, and the world at large. To break such norms was to skip gleefully past the point of no return, damaging so thoroughly one's reputation and standing in polite society that the disrespect would be palpable to all.

She then pondered where exactly the risk was to those who society had already decided did not belong. Did they—*she*—really have anything to lose by speaking the only language they seemed to understand?

Sometimes, undesirable behaviour was called for. If it was not just, it was at least warranted. *That* was a norm Kate could live by.

Chapter 14
Close your eyes and think of London

THE DAY of Franklin's soirée soon arrived, and with it, many people.

First came Franklin and Cécile. At the door, Franklin extended his hand, which Kate grudgingly shook. It was unfortunate that it had been her *other* hand she injured. He nodded *hello*, and with a glance acknowledged her injury.

Cécile blew straight past them, her craned neck steering her towards the grand hall. She gripped the corner of the door as she peered inside, but seemed disappointed by what she found.

'Catherine! Your grandfather's chairs, just shoved against the wall? Really!' She tutted. 'And it's too late now to move them! I suppose we will have to make do.'

Kate held up her injured hand, to wave at her mother.

'Oh, yes. Hello,' Cécile said, looking at Kate for the first time. And then, 'Is that what you're wearing? Please change into something more becoming, dear. Don't you have a nice dress you can put on?'

As the familiar words washed over her, Kate clenched her fists, causing fresh blood to seep from her wound. She excused herself as Cécile and Franklin milled around the grand hall.

After cleaning and patching herself up, Kate hid in her bedroom. She stood for some minutes in complete silence with her head against the door.

She had *one* dress, which she had not worn since her grandmother's funeral. It was plain black, knee-length, but not at all showy. She took a deep breath, counted to ten, and pulled it on.

In the grand hall she found that the caterers had arrived and were in the process of setting up. Franklin was busy directing them, and Cécile was flitting around with a duster. She caught Cécile's attention and motioned towards her dress. Cécile gave her approval by saying nothing and promptly returning to her nitpicking.

It was not long until guests began to arrive. First a trickle, then a cacophonous litany. They came in their grouped dozens, in their married and quarrelling pairs, in their hats, and in their Oxfords. They were stuffy and animated in equal measure.

Franklin stood by the door to greet them all with a strong handshake. From Kate—hands clasped firmly behind her back—they received a staid and slight bow.

As the masses invaded her home, Kate could

do nothing more than whisper quietly to remind herself why she was allowing this to happen. She tried her best to ignore the busybodies as they milled about, inspected her things, and measured between finger and thumb some speck of dust she had overlooked.

Cécile played the dutiful housewife. It was sickening. She sprung from guest to guest, enquiring after their needs, and taking on much of the waitstaff's work herself.

There came a point where, in her meandering, she happened upon Kate, who was idling by the wall. She shot her an instructive glare that seemed to say, *Make yourself useful, and don't you dare draw attention to yourself!*

All par for the course. Cécile was the type of parent who, with an only slightly misbehaving child, would, in the midst of a crowd of oblivious strangers, scream at the top of her lungs, 'Why won't you behave?! You're showing me up!'

Kate lost herself in the crowd. She slipped and squeezed between turned backs as she restrained sighs and muttered the occasional 'excuse me'. When she had embedded herself sufficiently deep into the crowd that she could no longer see Cécile, she felt a hand on her back. It belonged to Franklin, who pulled her into the group of men he was conversing with. There were three of them, and one looked suspiciously like the oil painting that hung nearby.

'It's a good likeness, don't you think?' he asked, motioning with a hand that held both a cigar and a glass of whisky. Smoke billowed above, and ash fell below. 'Commissioned by the bank for my twenty-five years, you know, and painted by the great —.'

Kate shrank in their presence, and sought a quick exit. But Franklin had decided now was the time to kiss the ring. His hand—still on her back—kept her in place.

He introduced her to the group: 'This is Catherine, my daughter. She's the current caretaker of Little House, which has been in the family for several generations. Of course we live at the much larger Bingingham Manor. Catherine, I'd like you to meet Messrs Harris, Owen, and Grant.'

One of the men—which one, she could

neither tell, nor bring herself to care about—extended his hand. She offered a light shake and a nod of the head. She then felt a tight squeeze —almost a pinch—on her shoulder. She had intended to conveniently forget Franklin's instruction, but the intensity of his grip made it easier to acquiesce and dip into a curtsy than to resist and continue her silent protest.

Determined for the evening's obligations to be over and done with, she greeted and curtsied to them all in turn.

Greetings concluded, their conversation immediately returned to the painting. The renowned artist behind the portrait had died shortly after completing the piece. They speculated that the subject may even have been the last to sit for the ill-fated genius. What was the painting worth? Possibly it was priceless. Another of the artist's portraits had recently fetched more at auction than most folk would earn in their entire lives. When he retired in three years, the subject planned to accept the painting as a retirement gift from the bank—he had even chosen where it would hang in his house.

Not a single subsequent glance was cast upon Kate, and she managed to slip away undetected.

The soirée seemed to be progressing as well as Franklin might dare to hope. From a safe distance, Kate observed the capitalist ritual in all its gory detail. It was a peacock dance; equal parts self-deprecation and flattery. It was shameless, spineless ingratiation. If Franklin's goal was to grease the wheels of his return to London society, he was surely succeeding. Of that, the frequent, raucous laughter from his quarters stood as evidence. With each compliment to the prowess of the men who could make or obliterate his dream, more heartily they laughed. And behind Franklin's glinting eyes and wicked smile, Kate saw loosening from its restraints the leviathan of ambition that would soon dictate the fortunes of others, as though he had not himself been a victim of such whims as recently as this night.

The soirée was almost over, and being satisfied that her errant daughter had more or less behaved herself, Cécile sought Catherine out.

'I think this has been a success,' she commented. 'All things considered.'

She looked Catherine up and down, wondering over her dress, her hair, and her makeup. The dress was nothing special, but it was at least acceptable. In many ways it was representative of Catherine herself: it was perfunctory, without a trace of elegance. Her hair was a mess; loose strands framed her face when they should have been tied back. And the less said about the makeup the better. *Less is more* was not always a maxim to live by.

Cécile brushed the loose hair behind Catherine's ears, cocking her head to judge whether it was a sufficient improvement. It would have to do.

'Now,' she said to her daughter, 'where is your friend Alfred?'

Catherine did not answer. Cécile felt that she was averting her gaze. That she was hiding something.

She prodded her: 'Well, come on girl. Spit it out.'

Catherine glanced around the room. In a moment of hope, Cécile thought she might be looking for her friend, to point him out. But no such luck. The search was in vain, and Catherine confessed that she had made a mess of things. How she could not manage something as simple as maintaining a friendship was astonishing. A psychologist could write a book about her!

Cécile's relationship with her daughter had been strained for some time—she knew that. But deep down she wanted nothing more than for her to be happy. And that, she knew, came from hard work, smiles, and patience. Whatever her Catherine had done to upset her friend, she could make amends. If she really wanted to.

She sighed.

'Where is he?'

Catherine shrugged. 'Probably at his precious art gallery.'

'Art gallery?' Cécile perked up. If only her Catherine could learn to appreciate art! 'Oh Catherine, if only you could appreciate fine art! So much better than those fusty, musty books.'

But Catherine did not engage as she hoped. She only offered: 'There's an exhibition tomorrow. Maybe you should go before you leave town forever.'

'An exhibition! Were you invited?'

Catherine sighed and nodded her head.

'Excellent!' Cécile clapped her hands with excitement. 'All you need to do is to swallow your pride, turn up, and say you're sorry. If you're lucky, he'll forgive you.'

'Mother, I don't think—'

Cécile cut her off: 'Do not question me, Catherine. Just do as I say. In fact...' and here she reached into her purse to produce some banknotes, 'buy something nice to wear. He's more likely to forgive you if you look nice.'

Chapter 15
Finishing touches

'WHAT ON EARTH HAPPENED TO YOU?'

Jane tapped the plaster that covered the bridge of Alex's nose. He flinched, and shook his head.

'An incident with a customer.'

The day of Jane's exhibition had arrived. Invitations had gone out, the artist was en route (travelling quite some distance, but due soon enough), and to the event she was applying the final touches.

Alex had kindly volunteered his day off to help with the final push. Jane probably should not have accepted his help, of course. She was unsure what the *insurance* situation would be if he, carrying out unpaid work, damaged something. But time was slipping away, and whether she liked it or not she needed the help. After a stern warning to be very careful, she put him to work.

The gallery was closed for the day, so they met mid-morning and worked until the first attendees began to filter in in the evening. Every second was precious. Even when taking lunch at the Cock & Bull they spent more time talking than eating, considering the best way to manoeuvre various items of furniture to get everything into place with the minimal amount of effort; a kind of Tower of Hanoi.

As they worked, Jane found herself wondering about Alex's wound. He was not keen to elaborate on the incident, and was evasive when she pushed him on it. It was not that she was incredibly curious to know the specifics; more that she was frightened of what they might be. It scared her that someone could come into his place of work and cause physical harm to him.

She wondered if she was viewing the incident from a position of privilege. Was it just a hazard of working with the public outside the high society of art galleries? She considered that perhaps it was: there was no shortage of signs warning the public that staff have a right to work without fear of being assaulted. But surely it was not a common occurrence?

A number of questions plagued her. Who had set out to hurt her friend? And was he reluctant to speak about it because it was traumatic? Or was it just so regular an occurrence that it was no different to any other day? She could not decide which scenario was worse.

Ultimately, she did not feel comfortable pushing him for details, even to assuage her own worries; their friendship was too new.

She asked about the day he had given up in

order to assist her. She hoped he did not have anything planned that he was now missing out on. Was he *sure* he was okay to be helping her?

He curtly assured her that he was.

He seemed to be a mixed bag of emotions. On certain subjects he was uncharacteristically stoic, and on others he was animated.

Some of the artist's least popular works were taken from storage. They would be put on display alongside the other pieces, in hopes they might finally sell. In carrying out this job, Alex was happy and helpful. He came up with wonderfully emotive blurbs for the paintings, and penned them in a far neater handwriting than Jane could hope to manage. He rather enjoyed this artist's work. He told her how much he was looking forward to meeting them. Jane had already added his name to the guest list, right at the top.

They continued to work hard, and in what seemed like no time at all the daylight had faded, the support staff had arrived, and the doors were due to open.

Jane was nervous. All of her hard work and planning would be put to the test. It was now too late to change anything. Would her carefully laid plans lead to an engaging and entertaining evening, or would they collapse like a soggy house of cards? Her mind rifled through the worst-case scenarios. Had the agency fobbed her off with substandard support staff? Would any of the art sell? If it was not a roaring success, would she be berated by the gallery owner? Or worse, would she receive a pat on the head and not be trusted with any future projects?

Her shoulders were tense, and her eyes darted from thing to thing. She was desperate to ensure all was perfect. Lost in her thoughts, she did not hear Alex call her name. When he placed his hand on her shoulder, she jumped back in shock.

'Don't worry,' he attempted to reassure her. 'All the planning, the hard work, the analytics... if anything goes wrong, all it means is you have something to learn from. It's not a case of *success or failure*; life isn't black and white like that. But, I think what you've done here is good. We hold events all the time across the road, so I'm not a stranger to planning things like this. You've got the food, the drink, the entertainment, and the people. There's nothing obvious you've forgotten. All you need is to greet people, keep things moving, and, most importantly, talk about the art. Trust me: you've got this.'

For a moment, Jane's shoulders relaxed. She exhaled a long, slow, steady breath, closed her eyes, and allowed a wake of serenity to wash over her. She smiled, and squeezed the hand upon her shoulder.

Maybe he was right. She had given it her all. She should believe in karma, not kismet. The night would be a roaring, unbridled success.

Chapter 16
Kate, Maggie, Anna

KATE DID NOT APPRECIATE Cécile's condescending tone, nor her nonsense platitudes. But when she considered her most recent interaction with Alex, she did feel a slither of remorse. Her message was clear, and her manner of delivery effective. But she had become the raging public spitting bile in someone's workplace. It was difficult to reconcile with her self-image. For that, at least, she possibly owed him an apology.

She had declined Cécile's money, and had not yet decided to attend the gallery exhibition. So it came as a surprise when she woke the following day and found, propped against her front door, a carefully wrapped and boxed evening dress. She brought it inside and immediately cast it aside.

By the afternoon, after much self reflection, she made the decision to find Alex at the gallery and apologise. She would be in and out, but she would be damned if she would go sober.

A sizeable glass of whisky later, when she

was sufficiently prepared, she considered the box, and her mother's gift that lay within.

Curiosity got the better of her. She pulled on the dress and looked at herself in the mirror.

She wore it well, but that was no good thing. It was the kind of dress the women she hated wore. She tore it off and threw it to the floor.

She pulled on her funeral dress, dragged a brush through her hair, and took a final sip of liquid courage before setting out.

After a brisk walk in sensible shoes, Kate found herself stood outside the art gallery, shivering in the bitter cold. Her hair blew every which way in the wind.

On the door, a youngster was checking the names of guests as they arrived. He looked too young to have a job. *Probably someone's nephew,* she thought.

Kate took a sideways glance at the list while he checked off the names of the couple in front of her. There was no *Maggie*. She would have to get creative. But at least Alex had not been so foolish as to put her name down.

It was still early, so plenty of folk had yet to arrive. Kate spied an *Anna* whose identity she thought she might assume.

'Name?' the youngster asked.

Kate brushed her hair aside and cooly answered: 'Anna. Anna Smith.'

Her latest false name was dutifully checked off, and she was shown inside.

The warm air hit her like a rugby tackle. Her body, previously tense from the cold, enjoyed a tingle that began in the small of her back and spread into an all-over shudder.

A glass of champagne was offered to her.

Yes... I'll be needing this, she thought.

She tilted back her head and downed the drink, handing back the empty glass and plucking a fresh one from the serving tray.

Kate waltzed forth, observing those around her and how they conducted themselves. How ridiculous they were; dressed a certain way, talking a certain way, suffering through hours of self-imposed falseness when they could just as easily be their own comfortable selves. And for what? The approval of their fellow poseurs? Some shred of social credibility? Rather them than her!

The gallery had a peculiar layout. Kate was used to art galleries with superfluously large rooms, wasting copious amounts of space. But this gallery felt more like an antique bookshop, with multiple rooms and anterooms coming off the reception area in which she stood (the only spacious room she could see). Even here, every surface contained something to look at. It was horribly overcrowded. It was overwhelming.

She downed her second glass of champagne.

The main action, it seemed, was taking place in the room directly ahead. Perhaps in there she might find Alex and then be able to escape.

As she made her way through the crowd, she was cornered by two older women.

'Oh, aren't you gorgeous!' exclaimed the first.

'Yes, beautiful!' replied the other.

'It is so refreshing to see you young people here, showing an appreciation for art. People these days just don't appreciate art anymore. It's not like in our day, when children were brought up with respect. Tell me, dear, was it your parents' influence that made you an art lover?'

Kate snatched a third glass from a passing waiter and took a large sip, considering her options. She was sure she had heard that the quickest way to disarm someone was to do something unexpected. So what the hell?

She adopted a Transatlantic accent and replied: 'Well, of course daddy was a great supporter of the arts. R— and M— were always entertaining with us at the manor.' She name-dropped two contemporary artists her mother used to talk about. 'But I didn't share his passion for the new art. I prefer the old masters, don't you know?'

'How wonderful!' one of the women—it did not matter which—exclaimed. 'Did you ever meet...?' She nodded her head to a nearby painting. The big famous painting they kept in the window to draw people in for the old bait and switch.

Damn, it had only encouraged them. *Where was Alex?* She would have to dial it up a notch. She took another large sip.

'Oh, of course!' Kate lied. 'Several times. Of course, their talent for art exceeds their talent for humour. Had a habit of telling the most awful jokes, don't you know?'

She threw back her head to laugh obnoxiously, then threw it back once more to finish her third glass of champagne.

🐌

'...of course, during that period the artist worked in seclusion, producing some of her finest pieces.'

Jane was surrounded by a group of tourists who had happened upon the gallery on the way to their hotel. She had decided to allow them in, as a member of the group purported to own one of the artist's earlier works, back home in the States.

Tourists comprised a sizeable percentage of the gallery's visitors. Perhaps even the majority. Some were art lovers; some were just on a mission to cram as much 'culture' into their visit to England as possible. On an average day, there were plenty from each camp, and Jane had learned to tell them apart with reasonable accuracy.

Alex approached the group and listened to Jane's discourse about the artist. When she finished speaking—and before anyone else from the group could continue the conversation—he pointed at a painting across the room and asked, 'Excuse me, miss. I wondered if you could tell me more about this piece?'

'Of course,' Jane said with a smile. 'If you'll excuse me, gentlemen.'

They removed themselves to the painting in question.

'*Thank you,*' she sighed.

She enjoyed talking art, but when someone latched on and would not relent, it could be exhausting. Even with topics on which she was passionate. And especially when all they really wanted was to hear the sound of their own voice passing off their amateur opinions as those of an expert. It happened more often than not. But it was part of her job, and she loved her job. Warts and all.

She took the opportunity to rest briefly against the wall to recharge. But the respite was short-lived: from the next room, an almighty clang rang out.

'Oh hell!' Jane exclaimed.

She raced off, but before she made it ten paces one of the guests collared her with a question. A member of the support staff nodded at her to indicate that all was under control, and she sank into the next long-haul conversation. She wondered, briefly, if this was something she should have planned for, and whether it could have been outsourced.

'Argh, hellfire rising.'

On the floor before Kate sat an upturned tray. A crowd had gathered around her as her stories grew wilder and wilder, and, with them, her gestures. At some point she had knocked a serving tray clean off the hand of a waiter, sending it tumbling to the ground and scattering hors d'oeuvres everywhere.

The waiter scrambled to clean the mess. Fortunately, the tray had been almost empty. As he worked underfoot, Kate sheepishly and silently sipped from her umpteenth glass of champagne.

After Jane was freed from her latest conversation, she decided to check on what had happened in the other room.

She found a member of the support staff working diligently to clean a small mess on the floor. Stood nearby were a group of guests. From behind, Jane could see that they were all older individuals, save for a single young woman.

The woman wore a nice dress, and with a bracketed arm held aloft a glass of champagne in a manner that screamed *socialite*. Jane thought she recognised the man stood next to the woman: Colonel Wilson, a wealthy, retired, military man. He was well-known for his taste in art significantly older than himself, and for women significantly younger. The young woman stood next to him, Jane therefore assumed, must have been his latest dilettante.

Nothing further requiring her attention, she returned to find Alex.

Alex was used to enjoying the gallery in silence, as an escape from work—not with all the hubbub that now filled it.

Seeking a moment's peace and quiet, he retired to one of the viewing rooms that were dotted around the edges of the gallery. They were each partitioned with glass, and featured a comfortable sofa, a fully stocked bar, and adjustable mounts and lighting.

Jane had taught him about the hidden beauty of each painting that only raking light could unlock—how the minute shadows cast by the paint's impasto could fundamentally alter the essence of a picture. A painting of a couple enjoying a walk outside could depict a quiet evening stroll or a midday promenade, depending on how it was lit. The skilled artist could intentionally create such dynamics in their works, and, as with most things in life, pulling this feat off was not as easy as it looked.

The room was dark. The din of the event, which Alex had helped orchestrate, roared dully on beyond the glass door. He sat on the sofa, leaned his head back, and closed his eyes. His mind turned to Maggie.

It's a shame I couldn't convince her to come, he thought. *After that ordeal with her parents, it would have been a good for her. But perhaps it's for the best.*

He thought back to the other day, and still could not understand what had gone wrong. She was hanging onto him, making conversation, laughing, and then turned on a sixpence. The clean-up after her histrionics was not so bad; the mop and bucket were most days on the floor, and not a night passed when at least one glass was not dashed into a hundred pieces. It was the swiftness with which her temperament changed that had him at a loss. What had he said?

But his silent contemplation was short-lived. The door flew open and his body rocked like a boat on turbulent seas as someone plopped down next to him.

Landing most unceremoniously beside him was a young woman who, in one hand, clutched a bag, and, in the other, a half-full glass that splashed over them both.

'Oh dear! Sorry, I didn't see you there,' she exclaimed.

He smiled at her politely.

'Sarah,' she said, by way of introduction. She held out her hand.

Sarah wasted no time diving into unsolicited conversation. The topic was *school*. This wasn't so unusual. Younger folk frequently spoke of their school days: the mischief they got up to, who was now doing what, and which scandals had hit which now-disgraced teachers. But *school* was such a subjective topic that it was truly meaningless to anyone peering in from the outside.

Sarah had kept in touch with *everyone*, Alex was told. But at the same time, she was surprised to learn that the quiet girl she never had time for was now in charge of this gallery. It was suspicious that she had not been on her radar. Though 'fair play' for doing alright for herself.

The drudgery of conversation continued for several more minutes before the door once more flew open.

Another woman joined them. When Alex turned to look, he saw Maggie. And he was floored: not only had she turned up, but she looked *nice*. If not somewhat lacking in balance and social graces.

His thoughts surfaced immediately as words: 'Wow, you scrub up well!'

Her initial smile turned to a frown.

'That is not the compliment you think it is,' she said flatly.

The exchange did not go unnoticed by Sarah, who likewise turned to Maggie, and likewise recognised her.

'It's you!' she exclaimed, pointing a finger.

Maggie's eyes widened.

'Yes, we went to school together! Don't tell me, it's...' And several incorrect guesses followed.

Maggie cut her off.

'Yes, it's me,' she said. 'Hello Sarah.'

Sarah lost no time diving back into stories of their time together at school.

'Do you remember the pranks we used to play?' she asked.

'I remember being barricaded in the art room overnight and getting a bladder infection.'

Maggie's expression was stern.

'Oh, you were out within ten minutes! Are you still in touch with any of the old gang?'

Maggie narrowed her eyes. A rage seemed to be building. Alex glanced nervously at the champagne glass in her hand.

It was at that point that the door opened once more, and a fourth person entered.

Maggie swung round.

'And just who the hell are *you*?' she demanded. Then fell into silence as her glass slipped from her hand, and muttered, 'Jane...'

There, before Kate's dumbfounded eyes, was Jane. Not the Jane who had of late been keeping Kate company at Little House, nor the Jane who had stopped Kate in her bloodied tracks on the high street—not that ghost of Jane; that idealised figment of Kate's imagination whose company and advice had helped her navigate an increasingly lonely world—but *Jane* Jane, her old friend, now here before her, real and in the flesh. Jane, who a year ago had disappeared from her life so suddenly and completely that she could only assume the worst.

Jane.

Part Three

Chapter 17
Just Kate

'KATE!'

How long had it been since Jane had last seen her old friend? It felt like half a lifetime. Discovering her here, now, at her debut gallery exhibition, Jane found a very specific version of Kate. Instantly recognisable, she saw before her *Drunk Kate*.

Kate had always held strong opinions about the vices of alcohol and of those who consumed it. But she was no stranger to the vice herself. In times of tragedy and unrelenting hurt, she would drink to distraction. It was nothing unusual—she would drink to numb her pain and lift her inhibitions, like everyone else.

At best, she became more passionate about everything: she laughed more, she loved more, and she cursed more. The glass of her life did not become half-full, but she would laugh riotously at tragedies about which she would otherwise cry.

At worst, she sank deeper into whatever

funk she was attempting to escape, until it became her singular focus.

Jane had lived through most of Kate's tragedies and subsequent escapes. She always had a front-row seat to the spectacular ebbs and flows of her mood.

At first, the highs were a welcome distraction from Kate's melancholy. She would laugh gleefully at (and even ridicule!) the absurdity of her situation. She would make crass jokes, and could even seem to forget her woes. But she could also be tactlessly critical of the faults of anyone foolish enough to wander into her line of fire. Whether friend or foe.

Jane, of course, made allowances for her friend to feel whatever pain she needed to feel, and to cope with it in any way that worked. For the longest time she took nothing personally, until the pessimism and anger far outweighed the precious relief, and Kate's altered states created more problems than they solved.

Jane found it increasingly difficult to keep up the dual roles of *friend* and *protector*. And, to her shame, she found herself caring less with each passing day about the woes of her oldest, dearest friend. She saw less and less of Kate, until eventually, around the time Kate's grandmother died, she stopped calling on her altogether.

It was not Jane's proudest moment. The only salve to her conscience was that Kate had similarly made no effort to remain in contact. And when she began to experience positive life events—new friendships and a promising career

—Jane could not help but think of all the ways Kate might have held her back and dragged her down.

Their abrupt reunion brought with it some seconds of silence. Kate appeared dumbfounded; her eyes were wide with shock. She was rigid, with arms outstretched at her sides. As she drifted off-balance, she propped herself back up sharply, in the way only the inebriated can.

'Wait... *Kate*?' Alex asked. 'Who's Kate?'

'Ohhhh noooo...' Kate whispered.

Her hands were now outstretched in front of her, as if pushing back obstacles in the dark. She looked slowly from Alex to Jane, and back again.

'Nooooo...'

'Maggie, I'm confused.'

'Maggie?' Jane questioned.

'Yes. This is Maggie.'

'Your new friend?'

'Yes.'

Jane was very confused.

'This is *Kate*. She's my best friend. At least... we were best friends in school.'

Kate suddenly piped up: 'Friend? Friend?! My life falls apart, and you disappear off the face of the earth! My world crumbles, and you swan off to art shows! You're not my friend! *I thought you'd died!*' She repeated those last words to herself, quietly.

'...what?' Alex questioned.

Kate turned to him and lashed out: 'Oh fuck off, Boy Scout. You broke into my house; are you surprised I gave you a fake name? Are you seriously that stupid? Or were you two in cahoots? Some sick game to twist the knife?'

She then turned to the other woman in the room.

'And *you*! I hope you die, you vapid sack of flesh.'

Silence fell. The tension was palpable. The other woman—Jane knew her to be an old classmate, married to one of the gallery's minor patrons—looked set to retaliate. But before another word could be said, Kate stormed out of the room.

'*Kate?*' Alex muttered to himself.

❧

Kate raced home, stumbling, pushing past children, and dashing recklessly across busy roads.

Tears streamed from her eyes as she began to process what had just happened. Jane had died. She *knew* she had died. Hadn't she? Why else would her best friend have so suddenly disappeared from her life? And yet, there she had been, alive and well, before Kate's unbelieving eyes.

She thought about their imagined conversations. Jane had always been the more pragmatic of the pair, and Kate found immense value in counselling herself in Jane's voice, imagining her there in times of need. It kept her grounded when she felt herself begin to spiral. It was the sanity check for her impulses.

Now that illusion lay in tatters. Jane was not her tragically absent friend and anchor, but the latest in a long line of those who sought to hurt her. It was an insidious betrayal, cutting deeper than any physical wound.

Kate wondered if Jane had been in league with Alex. He had come into her life so suddenly, and was so persistent in shepherding her towards the art exhibition, where the big reveal had taken place.

What were the odds, really, of all those people—including Sarah!—being in that room, at that time? It must have been carefully orchestrated so they could all laugh at her. The simplest explanation was, after all, almost always the truth, and that truth saw Kate once more suffering for allowing her guard down.

It seemed as though everyone had been keeping secrets. Jane could not understand how she, Kate, and Alex could all be so well acquainted with one another, and yet none of them realise it.

And what was it Kate had said to her? *I thought you'd died?* That knocked the wind out of her.

Of course, Jane understood. She never said *goodbye* to her friend. One day it had occurred to her that she was overdue a visit, but she could muster neither the energy nor the will to see it through. She did not actively decide to cut ties with her friend; she just postponed that next visit indefinitely. Kate, who never left her house, could be forgiven for assuming the worst.

There was also the matter of *Maggie*.

The scene unfolded with such rapidity that it was difficult to take in every detail, but Jane was sure she understood that Alex knew Kate under a different name, and that she had given him that false name after he broke into her house.

She paused in thought. Was that really something Alex was capable of? Kate could be justly accused of many things, but lying was not typically one of them. Alex's version of events turned out to be somewhat clearer: he had stumbled onto her land while rambling, had scared her, and offered to fix her broken fence by way of apology—everything that occurred thereafter had been serendipity. It was only the notion of Kate entertaining large groups and frequenting public houses that gave Jane further pause for thought.

Alex, when he learned the truth, seemed at a loss. Whatever he *thought* he understood of Kate turned out to be only a fraction of her true self. It fell to Jane to sketch in the areas about which Kate had been cagey—or just plain lying. She told him of the losses and cruelties Kate had suffered, including those she now realised she herself had inflicted.

The situation began to weigh heavily on Jane. Until their surprise reunion, she had been able to maintain some level of plausible deniability, as though she had not *actually* committed any sin against her friend. It was not until the consequence of both her actions and inactions stared her in the face that she felt their full weight.

'Has she always been this... erratic?' Alex asked.

Jane shrugged. That was a far too *black and white* way of looking at things.

'I understood that she had issues,' he mused. 'Hell, I met her parents. But the lies? I know I can come on strong. But that's just the bartender in me: you try to probe just enough that people crack and pour out their souls. It's supposed to be therapeutic.'

'You lot *actually* do that? Isn't that a bit old-fashioned?'

He laughed.

'We're an old-fashioned pub. It's actually one of the reasons certain folk come in every day. And having someone to listen to helps pass the time.'

They could have discussed Kate and the practice of modern bartending at length, but all around them the exhibition was still in full swing, and the artist would soon be speaking. *Kate in all her glory* would have to be a subject for another day.

Chapter 18
Reconciliation

THE SOIRÉE LEFT the grand hall in an untidy state. Things were displaced, surfaces were stained, and glasses were broken. An ugly hole now proudly sat where the offensive painting had been hastily hung and hours later removed. Chairs were scattered around and about.

In the midst of it all, Kate was sat in one of the nicer chairs. She had collapsed into it on her return from the gallery, having burst through the front door, torn off her dress, and pulled on a dressing gown.

It was pitch black, so except for the faint moonlight that shone through the window and illuminated a patch of floor, she sat in darkness, staring at the celestial body and the few twinkling stars she could make out through her teary eyes.

She eventually drifted off to sleep, and slumped in the chair.

As the heavens turned, the moonlight swept across the room. In time, the moon gave way to the sun, and dawn broke.

She was rudely awoken. First by the sun as it peeked over the woodland to stream into the grand hall. Then by an incessant knock at the front door.

'Kate?' came the now-familiar voice of Alex.

She rubbed her eyes and sat up straight.

What sick game is this? she thought.

Her hair, tousled as much from her desperate dash through the streets as from sleep, was all over the place. Similarly disturbed was the makeup that had felt the wrath first of her emotions, and now of her balled-up fists.

She determined that she would not be guilted into answering the door. Not to Alex. Nor to Franklin or Cécile, for that matter. Not even to the fellow who dropped off her groceries.

'Kate?'

This time it was Jane.

Kate leapt up with a start. She did not know what to do. Just a day ago, Jane at her door would have been cause for wild celebration. Now it filled her with confusion, misery, and anger. What was she doing here? And with the pretender, no less? Had her complete and utter gutting the previous night not been enough for them?

She closed her eyes, and desperately sought advice that did not come. She could no longer conjure a vision of Jane to dispense common sense. One more precious comfort she had been robbed of!

'Go away!' she screamed, after a further knock.

Jane did not relent. She continued to knock and to call out. Kate feared that she would have to answer. She knew Jane could be persistent. When they were younger, Kate had one day been tripped and twisted her ankle. At home, she hid in her room and would not come out. Cécile's attempts at coaxing her out were short-lived, soon giving way to anger and then apathy. But Jane did not give up: she knocked on Kate's door for two whole hours, until her friend eventually relented and let her in.

Reluctantly opening the door, Kate sounded as awful as she looked. Her voice was timid and cracking.

'Please,' she pleaded. 'Please... just leave me alone. I don't deserve this.'

She began to sob, and crumpled into a heap.

Jane caught her, stroked her hair, and shushed her. In an instant, they reverted ten years. Alex looked on, stupefied.

A cacophony of emotions screamed within Kate, all vying for supremacy, and all coming up short. They surged in parallel through her body, like adrenaline after the bark of a vicious dog, and burst to the surface in equal measure.

Her eyes sobbed and her body shook violently. Her legs offered no support. She would have been a puddle on the floor, were it not for Jane's embrace.

'Let's get you inside,' Jane said, motioning to Alex for help.

They walked Kate inside and sat her down

on the sofa. Her head sank between her knees and her hands covered her ears. She rocked back and forth gently.

'I thought you died,' she sobbed. 'You disappeared, and I thought you died.'

'I know,' said Jane, resting a hand on Kate's shoulder. 'I know. I disappeared, and I didn't say *goodbye*.' Jane sat down, as if to compose herself, and added: 'I owe you the truth. Though you might hate me for it.'

Kate said nothing. Her sobs had temporarily ceased, but her head was still buried, and her breathing laboured.

'We've known each other most of our lives. You were my first and my dearest friend. We grew up together, and we went through hell together. For most of that time, I couldn't have asked for a better friend.

'But over time, we grew apart. We had different experiences. You had the lion's share of tragedy, and I feel ashamed to say it, but as things went wrong for you and you struggled to cope, I found it more difficult to be your friend.

'You sunk so far into your melancholy that you couldn't see the light beckoning you out. You were inconsolable. And I *tried*, Kate; honestly, I tried. But I just couldn't rouse you like I used to be able to; the jokes didn't make you smile, the hugs and compassion offered no comfort... nothing I could do seemed to help even the tiniest bit. As you withdrew further into yourself, I began to question whether you even *wanted* to be happy again.

'For a while, I just joined you in it. I thought

that maybe what you needed was a companion to empathise as you worked through things. But it pained me to see you suffer and continue to slip as you did. And the more I tried to stick by you, the more I realised I was losing something of myself. And I know I only felt a slither of your hurt, but it was unbearable. So I ran away.

'At first, I just needed time off to recharge. A respite from being down in the trenches with you. Those were the odd days you didn't hear from me. And it helped, for a while. But I ended up having to take more and more time for myself before I could come back, until eventually... I just stopped. I told myself that you would call on me when I was needed. But that call never came. I don't know what I thought that meant. I feel awful, and all this is not an excuse for my behaviour, but it is the reason.'

Kate remained silent. She continued to rock gently, her head still between her knees. But she heard every word Jane had uttered. She understood now Jane's great betrayal: her greatest joy had come from throwing off the burden of her friend who, refusing to *just be happy*, was every day being crushed further under the weight of loss and unkindness. It was sadistic; no other word sufficed.

But Jane was right about one thing: their lives had diverged, and Jane had got the better deal of the two. She had friends, success, and *blistering happiness*. What possible joy could be left for someone like her, who already had everything? Other than the dark pleasure of manipulating others like marionettes? She had surely recruited Alex, directed him to Kate's home, and primed him on how to befriend her for their wicked purpose.

Kate said as much, directly to their faces. She rose resolutely to her feet, staring down at them, streaks dried down her cheeks, and a coldness in her eyes.

'No, Maggie—Kate!—that's not true!' Alex protested. 'These things you're imaging... they're just conspiracy theories!'

He stood, but Jane pulled him back down.

'Yes, they are!' Kate said, turning her gaze to him. 'They are *your* conspiracies against *me!*'

'That's—'

Alex began to speak, but was cut off by Kate, who stamped her feet and screamed: 'Get out! Get out! Get out!'

Alex looked ready to flee, but Jane remained calm. She rose to her feet, reached out, and clasped one of Kate's hands in her own.

'What I did was unforgivable,' she admitted. 'And I hate to admit that I might even do it again. You were always so much stronger than me. You were always brave enough to refuse to change in the face of injustice. I took the easy way out and played by everyone else's rules. But I paid a steep price.'

Kate snatched away her hand, and folded her arms.

Jane continued: 'I don't expect you to forgive me. But it fills me with joy to know that you opened up and let someone in. Even if this idiot—' and here she looked to Alex—'made a complete pig's ear of it. Please don't stop giving people chances.'

Kate's gaze remained fixed on Jane as she spoke, ignoring Alex entirely. Although her anger did not subside, Jane's appeals to her strength and bravery softened her stance, literally and figuratively.

She *was* brave. It was true that she would not be cowed into living her life by others' rules; no one would ever have that power over her. Life was unfair, and others were rotten. But that was *their* problem, not hers.

Jane had been weak. She had bowed to the pressures placed upon her and abandoned what truly mattered. All for the hope of a trouble-free life. *Do as we say and we'll stop abusing you.* That was no way to live. That was not Kate. She would never submit.

If someone desired her acquaintance—Alex or anyone else—it could only ever be on her own terms. To trust either of them again would be a big ask. Even if she believed every word they said, it only made their actions towards her slightly less awful.

But she would give it serious consideration. She had sought advice from Jane, and from Jane advice had been delivered.

Chapter 19
No good deed

'So... *KATE*...'

It felt strange not to be calling her *Maggie*.

Although two full weeks had passed, the surprise and shock of the revelations about Kate had yet to wear off; even to lessen.

Alex and Jane compared notes. In their shared understanding of Kate, not much differed, although Alex's picture of who and what Kate was was significantly lacking in detail. Jane filled in the blanks the best she could. But even with all he came to learn, he could not shake the feeling that *everything* Maggie had ever said to him had been an elaborate lie— Kate. Everything *Kate* had ever said to him.

They departed from Kate on uncertain terms. At length, Jane had managed to calm her down, but no resolution was forthcoming. Emotionally, Kate seemed in no place to tackle the big question that dangled, like the blade of a guillotine, over them all: *What next?*

For a full week, they did not have contact

with each other. It was not until Jane visited Alex one lunchtime at the Cock & Bull that they began to discuss everything that had transpired. He was relieved when he saw her walk through the door: as Kate's oldest friend, he worried that she might be forced to choose between them, and her lack of contact for an entire week had strengthened his unfortunate belief that he might never hear from her again.

He had not lost the one. But had he lost the other? Did he *want* to lose the other? Jane counselled him to reconcile with Kate, if she was willing. She was a good person, Jane insisted, in spite of her chronic pessimism. And for the entirety of their friendship, Jane had apparently never known Kate to humour someone as much as she had Alex. That might be a foundation worth building upon.

How exactly he might benefit from a continued acquaintance with Kate, Alex was unsure. Part of her allure had been dashed. She was no longer the mysterious young woman living in wild seclusion. Now, he knew the finest and most intimate details of *who* she was and what made her *how* she was. The appeal of progressively learning about someone —the general joy of falling in love—was now absent; she was bare, with nothing left to uncover.

It was perhaps his sense of guilt that eventually convinced him to reach out and make contact. He was still not sure what action he had been responsible for that had hurt her so, but he recognised his imagined part in the conspiracy that came so easily and instantly to her mind.

That was no way to leave things.

So it came to pass that, some days later, he once more found himself stood at her front door. It was early in the morning, and through clouds that had brought torrential rain the previous night, the sun attempted to peek. He stood, ankle-deep in watery mud, his fisted hand hovering before the door, ready to knock.

He hesitated.

A part of him felt that knocking on her door was somehow wrong. He recalled his previous entreaties, and how they had been received.

In the end, he penned a short note on a leaf from his sketchbook, and slid it through her letterbox. He requested her company, whenever she felt up to it, at the Cock & Bull. And if their paths were to never again cross, he was pleased to have known her.

If he was being honest with himself, he did not expect to see Kate again. And that thought carried with it some relief. There was something to a quiet life, after all. So it came as a tremendous surprise when, that evening, Kate strolled into the Cock & Bull, ordered a glass of water, and occupied her spot in the frontmost snug. Alex wasted no time bargaining an early end to his shift, and was soon sat gingerly opposite her.

'So... *Kate...*'

She met his eyes, but said nothing. After a few moments of excruciating silence, she offered a small nod of her head.

The silence continued for a further thirty seconds or more, before they both began to speak: 'I—'

Alex laughed nervously.

'Please, you go first,' he offered, with a gesture of his hand.

Kate cleared her throat and took a deep breath, as though she were about to dive into an inadequately rehearsed speech. Her face was devoid of any discernible emotion.

'I didn't go to the gallery because you asked me to,' she began. 'I stand by my melodrama one-hundred percent. You shouldn't have pushed me to go. But...' and here her voice betrayed some element of humility or remorse, 'once I sobered up, I felt bad about the glass I broke. And I think I also bled on your floor. I'm sorry if you had to clean that up.'

'Not me personally. But thank you. There's a little stain on the floor.'

'Hmm.' Kate did not look happy about this. She shook her head and resumed her neutral appearance. 'Sorry.'

The olive branch extended, Alex considered that she was likely awaiting an apology of her own. She had just given him a clue about the subject: he had been too pushy. He understood in theory, but in practice there didn't seem much wrong with the way he had tried to get her out of her comfort zone; it was just the kind of thing a good friend would do. So then what manner of apology would suffice? His past apologies—the solid, tangible, apologies of coming to her door, and fixing her fence—had been poorly received.

For not respecting her boundaries, he settled for a simple 'I'm sorry'. A curt nod of her head seemed to suggest that the apology had sufficed. He extended his hand for a shake, but she did not reciprocate.

Again, an awkward silence hung over them.

'How did it go with your family?' he eventually asked, choosing the only topic of conversation he thought she might readily engage in.

Kate remained silent for some further moments. She took a long sip of her water before answering: 'Hmm. I bowed in submission, shook greasy hands, and seethed through every piece of insulting life advice they threw at me. By the time everyone left, they'd made a mess of my home. But I think they achieved what they wanted.'

'So, London?'

'If Cécile's stupid smile was anything to judge by? Off they fuck.'

Alex grinned.

Kate seemed lost in thought as she continued: 'It's funny. You spend so long wanting something, and you think you know how it will feel once you get it. But now that they're this close to disappearing from my life forever? I don't feel any different. I thought I would feel *something*, at least.'

'You don't feel anything at all?'

'No. But perhaps it's too early. Maybe I won't feel it until they're actually gone. Until then, I suppose it's not real. Or maybe I'll just never be happy.'

Prompting her to talk about her family had worked. Kate was now speaking freely—albeit more to herself than to Alex. Little by little, she was opening up.

She continued to speak for some time about her hopes and plans for the future. Alex sat through it all, listening quietly and engaging with obvious remarks where appropriate.

When, some time later, she finished her glass of water, he asked if she would like another. Her response took him wholly by surprise.

'Yes. But I'll get it. What will you have?'

Alex shook his head and chuckled to himself as she disappeared to the bar. How quickly he had been able to melt her icy exterior. And by naught more than allowing her to lead the conversation.

Of course, he still had significant misgivings. On the night of the exhibition he felt as betrayed as he was sure she must have. A friend who was not a friend! In many ways, they had suffered the same shock revelation.

He was sat, musing over recent and current events, when a voice called to him.

'Alex Smith?'

He looked up. Stood in the doorway were two police officers. They were imposing figures, blocking all light from the door. One of them he thought he recognised—the police were often called out on the weekends or close to closing time, and three or four of them he thought he knew by sight. They were decent fellows.

'How can I help?' he queried.

No sooner had he asked, than he found out. One of the officers approached him and placed cuffs upon his hands.

'I am arresting you on suspicion of actual bodily harm against Catherine Harville. You do not have to say anything, but it may harm your defence if you do not mention when questioned something which you later rely on in court. Anything you do say may be given in evidence.'

Chapter 20
Out of patience

THE CHARGE against Alex was simple: Catherine Harville had been found by a police officer, wandering the streets, bleeding profusely, claiming she had been attacked by a local bartender. Eyewitness accounts and a trail of blood pinpointed the Cock & Bull as the site of the attack. Her testimony then confirmed Alex as the prime suspect.

Kate was visited by police the day after the incident. They repeated her original comments back to her (as best the officer that found her had recorded them) and sought clarity on the finer points.

She was initially reluctant to comment on the specifics. But when Alex was mentioned as a potential suspect, it all came pouring out: how he had, on multiple occasions, trespassed on her land, that he had been persistent in attempting to befriend her, and that he would not relent in his insistence that they attend a social event together. Indeed, their argument that day in the

Cock & Bull had stemmed from her inability to make him understand that she did not want to go.

On the cause of her injury, she said nothing. But she intimated that it occurred during an altercation with him and 'was his fault'.

After his arrest, he was questioned at length. He was unable to deny the majority of her version of events, other than the cause of her injury. He was then released pending further investigation.

He called upon Jane immediately. There was no one else to whom he could turn. Who else would understand what had just happened to him? Who might hear the charge levied against him and start from a place of assumed innocence? Only Jane could understand.

'I'm at a loss...' was all he could muster. 'What kind of person does that?'

It was the day after his arrest. They sat on a bench in the park near the high street. The park was the single piece of undisturbed greenery that punctuated the otherwise-grey sea of shops and unattractive urban accommodation. It was a popular lunching spot for the workers of the nearby retail and industrial estates. But in the chilly weather it was rather empty; just a few solitary wanderers, and a couple of retirees playing chess.

'It doesn't sound like her,' Jane thought aloud. 'She's not malicious.'

'Not malicious?! They reckon they've got me bang to rights for assaulting her! All I did was invite her to your exhibition!'

'And I bet she told you she didn't want to go. Am I right?'

Alex huffed.

'She made excuses. But she was in a good mood. Right up to the second she snapped and took a swing at me.'

On that point, he felt vindicated. Making friends was an imperfect science. There was nothing wrong with trying to push a friend outside of their comfort zone. She just had trust issues. After meeting her family, he understood some of the reason why. But it was not fair that she should miss out on so much in life, just because others' selfishness had taught her to suspect everyone's motives. She was an adult, after all! She could make her own fortunes. She just needed someone to give her a little nudge. That was not a crime. Even if he had been deeply disrespectful towards her, and an objectively bad friend, that was still not a crime!

It was ironic that, having gone through and come out the other side of a Kate Harville friendship, Alex's own trust was shot, like so many fish in a barrel. His patience was exhausted. Whatever progress he had made with Maggie, the chaos Kate had rained upon him made the prospect of further reconciliation a non-starter.

He was done with her. She finally got her wish.

❧

Jane had visited Little House many times over the years. But it was not entirely as she remembered. The flora had grown wild. And the facade of the house was in a particularly sorry state: flaking paint exposed grey, weathered wood; the sign that named the house was rusted, as were the screws that held it in place; window putty cracked and fell away. Alone, she took it all in.

And then she knocked on the door.

Tap. Tap-tap. Tap. Tap-tap.

It was a knock that Kate would recognise. It was their knock; a silly habit they converged on long ago.

Kate answered the door.

'Jane...'

The look on Kate's face made clear that she was aware what had happened—what she had done. But she did not appear wholly contrite. There was, for sure, remorse and sheepishness to be found on her face, but it was not without a dash of defiance.

On the subject of what had *really* happened, Jane preferred not to think that Kate had acted maliciously. Perhaps she had stated her version of events, and her reservedness had been taken as an unwillingness to point the finger where it deserved to be pointed. It was entirely possible for her to be innocent of the wrongdoing, while still ultimately its cause.

Jane walked inside and Kate followed. They turned to face each other. Both waited for the other to speak. Eventually, Jane yielded.

'I came to deliver a message from Alex.'

'Yes?' Kate asked, crossing her arms in front of her chest.

Jane reached into her pocket to produce a folded piece of paper. She offered it to Kate.

'A letter?' Kate scoffed. 'Who writes a letter?'

Jane said nothing. She just shook the letter at Kate, who rolled her eyes before taking it and beginning to read.

Jane had already read the letter. It was short, written as a courtesy more than anything else—he felt it would be poor form to disappear from her life without notice, given all that had happened with Jane. But lines had been crossed. Whatever relationship he had fostered with

Maggie, it was now unthinkable to pick up and continue with Kate.

'I half expected a declaration of love,' Kate reflected. 'Whatever. I don't need him.'

Jane remained silent. As Kate read, she had taken the opportunity to observe the interior of the house; to take in the state of Kate's hermitage. All around and about were small signs that the upkeep and maintenance of the once-great Little House had been neglected. The majestic paintings that adorned many of the walls had collected much dust, and cobwebs seemed to connect any two articles of furniture that were close enough. Even the bookcases, a recent addition, had attracted a significant layer of dust—Jane could determine exactly which books had been read by the tracks left on the shelf before them. On the surface, all was in a state of disarray.

'You have to drop the charges, Kate,' she eventually said.

Kate shrugged. 'The police are pressing charges,' she explained, 'not me.'

'Then tell them what really happened. Tell them that it was an accident. That they misunderstood you and made assumptions. That you were hurt and upset, and when they jumped to a conclusion you didn't correct them. You don't want Alex to go down for this, surely?'

'Don't I?'

For a brief moment, Jane felt the world drop away from her. A hand covered the shock on her face, and she took a step back.

Kate shook her head.

'Urgh, fine. I'll tell them what a horrible person I am. Are you happy?'

Jane was not happy. She could hardly recognise her friend. She was bitter and twisted beyond anything Jane had ever known, even in her darkest days. It had always been easy to understand Kate's misanthropy, but now it had become proactive. Petty, malicious actions were no longer the sole remit of those who tormented her.

Jane stepped up to Kate, gripped her tightly by the arms, and said: 'What happened to you? How did you get so broken? This isn't you. If you could just let someone in, you could be so happy. I know you could.'

Kate looked her dead in the eye, not blinking, hardly breathing.

'What happened to me?' she asked matter-of-factly. 'My best friend died.'

Chapter 21
Can people change?

For all of Jane's insight into Kate's state of mind, she found herself now in new territory. Never before had she been stuck on the outside, staring in.

Had the shift from reactionary recluse to nihilistic antinatalist been the result, at least in part, of Jane's so-called 'death'? Were Jane's own actions of self-preservation objectively harmful? Could one even *be* objective about such a thing?

Maybe. Maybe not. Jane learned long ago not to attempt to philosophise with someone whose lived experiences informed their position. Even worse if that held true of both parties. No one could win, and everyone would be worse off for the effort. She might not like or agree with the *Kate* that stood before her, but she understood that she was the product of the mores of others, and that she (though she hated to think it) may now be chief amongst those *others*.

'You don't have to push everyone away,' Jane pleaded. Opposing sides of her then fought

to either free or bury the words that eventually
followed: 'I could still be a part of your life. If
you just put in a little effort.'

'Effort?' Kate scoffed. 'Why should I have to
change in order to be happy? When other
people are the problem? *People* can change,
not me!'

'But they won't!' Jane pleaded afresh. 'Kate,
they won't change. Don't be so stubborn that
you condemn yourself to a life of misery
because you're too proud to just plaster on a
smile and put up with the same minor bullshit
as the rest of us. You're an adult; it doesn't have
to be *all or nothing*. You can walk away
whenever it gets too much. Just give people a
chance.'

'I've given people more than enough
chances. People are all the same.'

Jane sighed, then got angry.

'Damn it, Kate! No one's saying you have to
put up with toxic relationships. But the people
around you have to get *something* positive from
their interactions with you. *I* have to get
something positive from my interactions with
you. Otherwise everyone will just form the
same opinion of you they always have. You need
so little effort to change that, it's laughable! And
yes, it will cost you some discomfort. But if you
don't start pushing yourself outside your
comfort zone, you'll just spend your whole life
suffering on your own. You're miserable anyway
—why not get a little happiness for your
misery?'

'That's all fine and well for you to say, with

your perfect life. But things don't work out like that for me. They never have, and they never will. And even if they could, my question stands: why should *I* have to be the one to change, if it's so universally accepted that people are awful?'

'First of all,' Jane retorted, 'life hasn't been easy for me. You're so wrapped up in your bubble that you seem to forget we endured a lot of awful things together. I didn't grow up with warm and fuzzy feelings about people and places. My life isn't perfect. In fact, the things I do every day often fill me with dread. Working with the public? What sane person would want that? But I put up with the occasional awful person because it means I get to do something I love. It's a trade-off. That's what you do: you pay a price for things you love. But at the moment you're paying a price and not getting anything in return!'

Kate's gaze pierced through her. She was unwavering.

'And second?'

'And second,' Jane said with a heavy sigh, 'you have to realise that love and friendship are a two-way street. Some of the things you want, they won't, and more importantly, some of the things *they* want, you won't. It works if everyone makes accommodations. But if one person takes and never gives...'

'Yes? What *if* one person takes and never gives?'

Jane sighed again.

'Then there is nothing left for them in the

relationship. And after a certain point not even empathy, sympathy, or nostalgia are enough to keep them emotionally invested.'

'And then they fake their death.'

Jane became instantly incensed. She yelled again, louder than before: 'I did not fake my death! All you had to do was call on me, and we would have had an awkward conversation where it all came out. But you didn't. You just hid away. I no more faked my death than you did!'

'You have no idea how it felt when I realised what must have happened to you! How dare you tell me I shouldn't feel the way I did! That I'm just making things up!'

'But you're inferring intent where none exists!'

'Am I?!' Kate demanded. 'The whole world are confidence tricksters!'

Jane began to pace, holding her hands to her head and recalling all the feelings of her final days with Kate before unceremoniously disappearing from her life.

What was Kate even arguing against? She was lurching wildly between paranoia about others' intent and an unwillingness to show flexibility in a relationship. That she might *have* a relationship with someone—confidence trickster or not—had not been a point on which she had offered an opinion. It seemed that every argument Jane employed to convince Kate of one thing triggered strong feelings on a semi-related topic, to which the conversation immediately pivoted. This was exactly the kind of philosophising she normally knew better than to engage in.

Exhausted from the confrontation, Jane collapsed into a nearby chair.

She felt intense sorrow for Kate. To see how far her old friend had fallen into pessimism; how completely bereft of hope she had become. She wished more than anything to be able to pull Kate from her pit of despair and help her see the light.

But more than anything else, she had lost the will to fight.

'I just... Kate, I'm here. If you want to be friends again, I'm here. We'll get away from everything and go see the stars. But you have to meet me halfway.'

Jane had given Kate a lot to think about.

The previous day's conversation had been exhausting. Jane was all over the place, and couldn't seem to answer a single concern without lurching off on some unrelated topic.

Kate wanted to imagine the advice Jane would have given her, but again could not summon the idealised vision of her friend. It was, ironically, now *she* who was dead.

She knew that the central piece of advice—*make small accommodations and you will be happier overall*—was sound. That was just common sense. But it was a bitter pill to swallow. The accommodations she would make would be to a world that had been so cruel to

her. There was honour in martyrdom, after all.
For those plucked from the void, noncompliance
was perhaps the most meaningful act in a
meaningless life.

But she had a serious choice to make, with
significant consequences for how she lived her
life. Should she patch things up with her best
friend who had pleaded with her for friendship,
making concessions that went against her
principles? Or should she stay true to her path
and eschew all that had ever caused her pain?

Kate reflected on her past with Jane. The
laughs, the games, the camaraderie, the support.
The betrayal. Their story was vast in scope; two
lives entwined, with soaring highs and plunging
lows; the stuff of epic poetry; heartbreakingly
special; heartbreakingly abandoned. Could a
heart once torn from the chest resume beating if
replaced?

She considered sleeping on it for a further
night, but in her heart she knew what she had
to do.

Printed in Great Britain
by Amazon